The Devil's Shadow

Book 2 of the Sister Witches

FELICIA JEDLICKA

For those who have been wronged.

More titles by FELICIA JEDLICKA

DESTINY REJECTED
DESTINY RECLAIMED
DESTINY RAZED
DESTINY RESTORED

DÉJÀ VU

SAVE THE HUMANS

THE NECROMANCER'S CHILD

SISTER WITCHES
THE DEVIL'S SHADOW
THE DEVIL'S SOUL

THE NEBRASKA APOCALYPSE NOVELS
CORN COWS AND THE APOCALYPSE
COW TIPPING AFTER THE APOCALYPSE
CORN HUSKING AFTER THE APOCALYPSE

THE WARDEN SERIES
SUCCESSORS
RIVALS
LOVERS AND LIARS
BAD BLOOD
TENANTS AND TYRANTS
THE RING BEARER
GODS AND MONSTERS
BEASTS AND BURDENS
MAGIC AND MAYHEM
FORK IN THE ROAD
DETAILS AND DEADLINES

The Devil's Shadow

Book 2 of the Sister Witches

FELICIA JEDLICKA

CHAPTER 1

C ANDLELIGHT SIFTED THROUGH THE screen in front of me, adding little glowing crosses to my face and chest. The profile of a man shifted into place on the other side of the barrier. After a moment, he cleared his throat.

"You may begin," he said.

"Forgive me, Father, for I have sinned," I recited. "It is been six months since my last confession."

"Yes, my child, what did you come to confess?" he mumbled.

I fiddled with the beads in my hands. I hadn't been one to find comfort in something as prosaic as a rosary, but in recent months, I depended on it as a measurement for how deep my soul had sunk. So far, the beads weren't burning my skin, so perhaps there was hope for me yet. "I am a minion of the devil, Father," I confessed in a whisper.

The priest shifted, glancing over to catch a glimpse of me through the screen. My appearance certainly didn't project an image of religious piety. Now that I was no longer a member of Sister Aggie's convent, I was fully embracing my black-tipped blond hair and my ever-present nose ring. I had given up my robe for a pair of black jeans and an oversized sweatshirt.

"I'm sure at times you feel you are being influenced by Satan, but surely—"

"I don't mean that metaphorically, Father. I am in the devil's service."

"Why do you think this?"

"It's a long story. I'm not sure you would have much sympathy for my situation if I tell you."

"Perhaps you could give me a summary of the events leading up to this evaluation of yourself."

"Well, you see, Father, until about six months ago, I was a member of a convent in a small town not far from here."

"You were a nun?" he asked, obviously not matching my style to this job designation either.

"Not exactly. You see, this particular convent specialized in serving the Lord in a more literal way. They performed ceremonies of witchcraft in order to heal the sick and exorcise demons."

"You seem to have been led astray, my dear. Nuns do not participate in these activities."

"No, not usually. This was a special group. Both nuns and civilians joined in a magically bonded coven. We carried out the will of God, using his miraculous power as the seed for our magic."

"What you're describing is heresy."

"I couldn't agree more, but the things they could do... It was amazing, Father. They brought me into the group. They accepted me, bonded with me, and taught me their ways. Unfortunately, the devil took notice. He didn't like that I was part of this group."

"How do you know he didn't like this?"

"Well, aside from telling me in dreams and visions, I was attacked by one of his alter egos. A lion."

"A lion?"

"The beast, Father. I have to admit, the stories of the devil are sometimes intriguing to me. I think it has something to do with human nature. Some part of us will always be curious and rebellious. But the beast, Father... There is nothing to romanticize about it. That is where his hatred lies. His anger and disgust at the human race reside inside the burning eyes of that mammoth creature." I shivered just thinking about the image.

"Was it the beast that forced you to become his minion?"

"No, Father, it was God."

The priest shifted again, no longer hiding the fact that he was staring at me through the screen. "You're saying God wants you to be the devil's minion?"

"Not precisely, but you see, I had an opportunity to kill him."

"God?"

"No, the devil. What I didn't understand about joining the coven, what I didn't understand about my parents dying; it was all because of him. He was drawing me in, tricking me into using my power. He wanted me so addicted to it that I would do anything to keep it. I was drawn to him."

"How did God come into play here?"

"Because I'm a part of the devil, the part of him that is a fallen angel. Anything that harmed me would harm him. I had a chance to sacrifice myself for the greater good. The gun was pointed at my head, a bullet in the chamber, my finger poised on the trigger. I even pulled it, but nothing happened."

"You believe God stopped you from shooting yourself?"

"If I'd shot myself, the last trickle of the devil's humanity would've died with us. All that would've remained would have been the beast and the ram."

"So, God saved you to save the devil. Why would he do that?"

"Because God still loves him. Also, he needs him. The devil's trinity was meant to be a mockery of God, but in a way, it has allowed the devil to focus his villainy appropriately. Violence to violence. Deception to deception. After all, it's not as if the devil seeks out good people to turn bad. He looks for corrupt people to make them worse."

"And where do you come into play? Don't tell me God needed you to babysit the devil."

I chuckled at that. It wasn't too far off, but at this point, it was very much the employer-employee relationship. "God gave me a soul."

"God gave everyone a soul."

"No, not me. My soul technically belongs to the devil. I was just missing a body."

"I don't understand."

"Neither do I really. I mean, it's all well and good to use the *devil's shadow* as a metaphorical definition, but the literal interpretation is that I was a broken fragment of his trinity. One he had never intended or permitted. I left him and hid in a body that didn't belong to me. I was not possessed; I was the possessor."

"You're saying the devil's soul developed an independent sentience that ran away and possessed a young woman?"

"Yes, actually, that's a pretty good interpretation, Father. I'm impressed. I've been trying to formulate that into words for months."

"How exactly did his soul develop a consciousness that could escape his body?"

"As you well know, free will lies in the soul. That part of the devil was still a creation of God, a hurt child, and a dejected angel. His pain was the seed of my existence. He pushed me away—those feelings—as far as he could, because they conflicted with his anger. The farther he pushed me away, the more independent I became. I couldn't stand watching the pain he inflicted and the anger in his retribution. I wanted out of hell. Out of him. Eventually, I had enough strength to separate entirely."

"So, you ran away, possessed a woman, joined a convent that was a secret coven. You had an opportunity to kill yourself, thereby killing the devil—or at least part of him—but God stopped you, and gave you a proper soul. And now you have two souls."

"Actually, no. God didn't give me a new soul, he just gave me permission to keep the one I had."

"I'm not sure I follow. If your being is the holder of the devil's soul, then the devil no longer has a soul."

"That's where it gets extremely complicated. You see, Father, God gave me permission to keep my soul—the devil's soul—in this body. Which means I'm protected as any other human would be from the devil, more specifically the beast. However, since this is his soul, I am still permanently connected to him."

"What exactly does that mean? I mean, in terms of impact on you."

"It means I have access to the devil's power, but he can divvy it out as he likes, for a price."

"And I suppose the price of that power is you becoming his minion."

"Precisely right, Father. Having access to this level of magic has changed me more than I would like to admit. The truth is, I'm basically an addict, turning tricks—so to speak—to get my next hit."

"That is a problem, my child. One I'm not entirely sure I can help you with."

"Oh, that's all right, Father. I didn't come here to get help. I only came here to confess."

"My dear, as complicated as all that is, I'm not sure you can claim any responsibility for your actions at this point. You're basically a slave."

"I agree, Father, but I wasn't coming here to confess my past sins. I came here to confess my future sins."

"That's not exactly how it works."

"No, not usually, but I wanted you to understand why I'm going to kill you."

The priest once again turned and looked at me through the screen. "What did you say?"

"It's an unusual duty, one I was very much against, until he explained the reason for it. I have no wish to be a murderer, Father, but I also have no wish to see a pedophile continue to desecrate the cloth for the sake of unnatural desires."

"That's a ridiculous allegation. I am not a pedophile." He slid the screen back into place and I heard the door to the confessional open and slam shut.

I chuckled as I sat in the confessional a moment longer. There was something poetic about the way life had turned out for me. I always had a knack for knowing when people were speaking truthfully to me. It was accurate to the point of being psychic. With or without magic flooding through my body, I could always know when somebody was lying to me.

And the priest was lying to me.

Chapter 2

I felt dizzy as I came down out of my magical euphoria. I couldn't deny my addiction to the power I drew from the devil. Since my official title change from black-eyed uber witch to the devil's bitch, my cravings for his flavor had reached new heights. Besides the aphrodisiac, Zen-energy cocktail he normally provided, my encounters had tipped deeper into the erotic end. I would do almost anything to get another dose of magic swimming through my veins like liquid evil.

Of course, I would never harm anyone who didn't deserve it in some way or another. I had established early on that I would only use my powers against bad people. However, there was no sugar-coating the work I did. I was an errand boy, and a hitman rolled into one.

I stumbled down the aisle of the church, stepping over the priest's downed body. I could barely see through the interior sunglasses of my oil-slicked eyes. My body had at least accepted the magic enough not to bleed out of every orifice after my performance. I still wasn't sure it was healthy for me to house the fuel of angelic rage inside a human form, but obviously I had stopped caring about that a while back.

I had stopped caring about a lot of things. Six months ago, I was part of a group that believed in doing God's will through magical intervention. I wasn't sure they kicked me out solely on the basis that I was using power from the devil. I think they finally kicked me out because they realized there was no distinguishing between him and me in my magical haze.

As disappointed as I was with their decision, I couldn't blame them for it. I knew it was scary as hell for them to watch me feed off of the energy I received from him. There was nothing pretty about black magic.

I stumbled out of the church, back into the downpour outside. It had been raining all week. I wasn't sure what was going on with the bad weather lately. It seemed to follow me around on my worst days. Rather than wait for it to let up like a normal person, I ran across the street through deep puddles to get to my car. I jumped in and started it up. I turned up the heater even though at that point I was sopping wet and even the warm air felt cold.

I turned on my windshield wipers and jumped at the sight of a man standing in front of my car. I recognized the broad shoulders that gave his body a perfect V-shape. Much like me, he had forgotten to bring an umbrella and was standing out in the rain, getting drenched.

It shouldn't have surprised me that he was there, but it always did. I hadn't told him where I was going. We hadn't even spoken in weeks. Not that we usually had very stimulating conversations when we saw each other.

I suppose I had to consider him my boyfriend, but that had also gotten complicated in the last six months. As if my existence wasn't already bordering on the line of good and evil, threatening to pour over into the evil part. Dane

Pratchett, formerly known as "Pratchett the Hatchet," was an ex-serial killer.

A very arduous blood ceremony eliminated most of his murderous ways, leaving him stricken with guilt for his crimes. I couldn't completely describe him as healed, since it was necessary for him to bear the penance of his painful abusive memories in order to keep him from acting aggressively against women again.

He was still very much capable of violence, but only to serve as my protector. He, unlike me, could see demons and touch them, which meant he could fight them and kill them. He was a nifty little stalker to have since apparently every demon in hell had heard about my promotion to the devil's right-hand gal, and wanted to possess me.

I had thought my evil other half would protect me from such intrusions, but he seemed to find great amusement in watching me toil my days away, fighting off the pesky parasites. He was a jerk like that.

My heart thumped a little harder as I stared out at Dane and considered my options. Option number one was letting him into my car. This would inevitably result in me driving him to my house and then sleeping with him. Option two was driving away and leaving him out in the rain. This option was probably the safest. If he had to walk home 40 miles in the rain, then he would certainly be too cool to try to warm my bed. Option three was shifting my car into drive and running him over. It wasn't really an option I wanted to take, but the thought popped in there nonetheless.

I shifted the car into reverse and backed away from him. He walked after the vehicle, as if he couldn't believe I was going to leave him in the rain. I caught a glimpse of him shaking his head as I drove off down the street.

A couple of blocks later, I glanced back to see if he was chasing after me on foot, but the only man I saw behind me was my employer. I frowned at the pretty boy face in my rearview mirror, his sculpted beard surrounding his smug smile. The perfectly coiffed black hair, and his skintight suit, reflected his vanity as well as my own. There was something weirdly inappropriate about being attracted to someone who was essentially a part of yourself. There weren't enough psychologists for that particular lapse in Freudian analysis.

"How did it go?" he asked, though I was certain he could feel every last bit of my post-murder high.

"He's dead," I answered. "Go see for yourself if you want."

"I don't doubt your thoroughness. That's not what I meant, anyway. I mean, how did you enjoy me tonight?"

I rolled my eyes, trying not to think about the potency of tonight's strangely sensual experience in magic land. "Same old, same old."

He cocked his head back and laughed. "Do you really think you can lie to me? If I can't lie to you, you can't lie to me."

"Why do you have to make this situation so... uncomfortable?"

"Oh, was that you being uncomfortable? I thought you rather enjoyed having my strength coursing through you."

"You were right. He was a pedophile," I said, changing the subject.

"Of course he was. Even if I could lie to you, what would be the point?"

"I don't know. To make me hurt someone who doesn't deserve it."

He clicked his tongue and scooted up close behind my seat. He brushed his finger down my cheek—though it technically never touched me, I could still feel his contact like a shiver or tickle. "Now Hennie, don't you know by now I care about you?"

"I know how selfish that sounds now."

"It's true. Ours is an unusual relationship, but I consider you to be like a daughter to me."

"Child of Satan? I'm moving up in the world. So, why do you keep placing your magic with titillation? Because I'm like the daughter you never molested?"

He chuckled again. "Speaking of molestation, I might have another job for you coming up."

"Another good deed? Two in one week. Is my birthday coming up?"

"No, but I reached maximum capacity on my amusement with this one. Besides, he's starting to believe God will help him overcome his desires if he prays hard enough. I want to show him God stopped listening to his prayers a long time ago. He should have prayed to me. I might've actually been able to help him."

"Would you have?"

"Of course. I would've held down his daughter for him."

I whipped my head over to glare at him. "That's disgusting!"

"Humanity is no better than a bunch of horny hunting dogs. It's not my fault you're such a weak-willed species."

"Well, maybe we would've been a little stronger if God's first creation hadn't turned out to be a dick. I mean, that kind of throws off the model for a while, doesn't it?"

I glanced from him to the road, seeing his smug smirk turn downward into a snarl. He leaned forward, pressing his lips to my ear. "Don't press your luck. Or I'll show you how much of a dick I can be for you."

I gritted my teeth as his tongue traced the rim of my ear. Again, he never made contact, but I still felt his power pushing through our connection. It demanded my body's undivided attention. When he had made his point, he pulled away and disappeared, leaving me to lament so many of my life's challenges, none more pressing than my sketchy and wavering libido.

CHAPTER 3

I STEPPED THROUGH THE door of what could hardly be considered my childhood home. My parents had been up-and-comers in the world of residencies. They switched homes three times during my childhood, each time getting a bigger and better home. They intended this house to be their retirement home, but neither lived to see that day. My mother died when I was in grade school—a car accident. Cancer took my father from me shortly after I graduated high school. However, as I understand now, neither of those incidents were the coincidental tragedy I'd thought they were. I knew now the devil had been plotting against me. He'd wanted me alone, desperate for companionship and guidance.

What he didn't plan on was Sister Aggie. A nun, blessed and gifted by God with foresight, brought me into the ranks of her *sister witches*. It was there I discovered my powers, and how to use them. I was so enamored with my abilities, I never thought to question why I had them.

Sister Aggie's foresight had ultimately brought me enlightenment about my true identity. The dirty little secret about the origins of my creation. She made the ultimate sacrifice to protect me and the other sisters against demon attackers, demons that would love nothing more than to ride on the backs of powerful witches.

Since I was now essentially the most powerful witch in existence, I was receiving more than my fair share of demon attacks. Since I couldn't defend myself in my sleep, I had taken to using old-school hexes.

I punched in the numbers on the security system and reinforced the pentagon on the back of the door. I mimicked the painted design with my hand and murmured a spell to ensure that anyone crossing my threshold did not intend to harm me.

I touched the wooden crucifix hanging in the center of the design and asked God to continue to protect me. As a borrowed soul in a confiscated body, I was far from the realm of God's good graces. However, he had seen fit to allow me this far. The question I didn't want to ask was how far he would let me go. I got the sense that God's will was the only thing that could stop me now.

I dropped my keys into a bowl on the table behind the door. Picked up a partially used sage blunt, and lit it. I searched the house, all the while spreading the protective smoke. Once I determined everything to be safe, or at least as safe as it ever was for me, I put out the sage and headed upstairs for an overdue shower.

I stepped into the long bathroom and looked into the only functional mirror in the house. In a fit of rage, I had broken several of them, and blacked out the others with spray paint. I'd even gone so far as to spray a frost glaze over the framed pictures of my family, so I didn't have to see my shadow's reflection in them.

I removed my earrings and slipped my sweatshirt over my head. I noted the deep hollow of my collarbone before removing my pants. I turned sideways in the mirror, examining the divots between my ribs and the concave drop where they met my stomach.

One of the side effects of my magical use seemed to be perpetual weight loss. This, of course, was any girl's dream, but unfortunately, I hadn't exactly been robust to begin with. The needless drop in weight was making me look gaunt. Even my face was looking a little sickly with its hollowed-out cheekbones and dark circles around my eyes.

Add to that the premature cracking in my back, and the persistence of my adult acne. I knew it was only a matter of time before I would be bent over, pockmarked, and frail as glass. Ironically, a truer image of a witch, one that apparently the devil would not let me escape.

I slipped out of the rest of my clothing and jumped into the shower. I wouldn't be able to wash away my concerns, but at the very least, I could smell a little nicer.

When I was through, I opened the bathroom door and smelled something burning. I cursed my luck and reached for my magic. Bundled up in my fluffy black bathrobe, I trudged downstairs to face the insidious rabid beast that had become the bane of my existence. I had hoped my servitude to the trinity would ultimately reduce the beast's rage for my existence, but it seemed to have the opposite effect. Both of the devil's branched personalities, the beast and the ram, had taken offense to my exalted liberation, and since they couldn't take it out on God, I was the next best thing.

As I crept down the hall, nearing the source of the smell, I realized it wasn't the fiery hands of a hell beast causing the odor so much as Dane's ineptitude in the kitchen. I released my grip on my power and leaned into the doorway of the kitchen.

The gourmet kitchen had a large island donned with hanging pots and a smoke hood. Dane had managed to get the hood turned on, and it was drawing most of the smoke outside. He was still beating his potholder on the stovetop, trying to tamp out the last of the embers on the cloth.

When it was finally out, he looked over the charred apple fabric and cussed at himself. He shifted over and looked at whatever he was frying in the pan. Judging by the frown on his face, it was obvious he had burned it beyond recovery.

I sputtered out laughter as I watched his face contort into a boyish pout. He looked up at me. His pout turned more fearsome, and he clenched his jaw. "I wanted to surprise you."

"By burning down my house?" I smirked at him. "That *would* be a surprise."

"How do you cook on this thing? There are more goddamn dials than an airplane cockpit."

I laughed. "My mother wanted a gourmet kitchen. According to her, this was a gourmet stove. At least, it was about a decade ago."

He grunted a response and moved his frypan over to the sink. He poured water into it, making it sizzle and steam. When the crackling was done, he set it down in the sink to soak and turned the water off.

"Why are you cooking, anyway?"

"It's not as if I can take you out to eat." He shrugged. It was true he couldn't. Dane's most notable trait was that he was wanted by the police—and the FBI. Given the strange manner in which he'd disappeared from his imprisonment, law enforcement was taking a rather heavy-handed approach to tracking him down. Even with my protection spells in place, it was only a matter of time before someone recognized him and reported him.

It was one of the many reasons I wasn't sure whether being in a relationship with a serial murderer was a good idea. I could argue with myself all day about the trauma that had inspired his acts of murder. I could also rationalize the forced recovery that had opened his mind to the suffering of his victims and allowed him to feel the proper guilt of a remorseful man. In the end, however, my mind always came back to one thought: he was a killer.

I supposed now I was also a killer. Where did I draw the line? At least he was a reformed killer. I was still currently in the business.

"You're cooking a meal for *me*?" I clarified.

"Yes. You need to eat."

I smiled at his concern. He did have the overbearing protection thing down pat. Since I had left the convent behind, he had voluntarily come with me. At first, I had thought it was due to our mutual attraction, but even after I started denying him my bed, he persisted to watch over me, day and night, without reward.

It was only recently that I interpreted his protection as a form of repression. And since he refused to leave my side voluntarily, I started to ditch him. Which was pointless, since he always found me. He had an uncanny ability to track me down.

"How did you get in?"

"Hide a key," he answered sardonically. I perked a brow at him and he shrugged. "I picked the lock."

"The alarm."

"I've watched you punch it in a dozen times. I know it by heart." He crossed his arms. "Why don't you ask me how I got here so fast? Or maybe you don't care that I had to ride in the back of a truck with three dogs and their fleas."

"You hitch-hiked?" I scrunched up my face in disappointment. "Dane, you know how dangerous that is."

"Then don't leave me on the side of the road."

"Stop following me and I won't have to leave you."

"Stop running away and I won't have to follow you."

"I'm not running away. I'm doing my job. The job I have no choice but to do. Which has nothing to do with you."

"That has everything to do with me!" he bellowed, making me tense. The anger in his face turned to shame, and he took a breath before speaking. "You need protection."

"Did you miss the part where I became the most powerful witch on earth? Imbued with the devil's power? I'm pretty sure I can handle myself against a few bad guys and some lackey demons."

"I didn't say you needed protection from someone else." He glared at me, his jaw rolling with dissatisfaction.

I stared at him, only beginning to glean his meaning. "Is that why you came with me? Are you still hunting me, Dane?"

He frowned and looked away from me. "You were never meant to be one of the good guys, Hennie. And neither was I." He looked back at me, his hard stare scolding me for my very existence.

"I can't help what I've become," I whispered.

"Neither can I," he answered back. "But I'm controlling it." He moved away from the counter and stepped into the doorway with me. He looked me over from head to toe. "Are you kicking me out tonight?"

I took in a breath and looked over at the messy kitchen. He had made such an effort. It was almost romantic. Romance wasn't something that usually came into our relationship. I supposed I at least owed him something for that. "I'll order a pizza."

Chapter 4

"STOP!" I SQUEALED AND yanked my foot back. Dane snared it in his grip and threatened me with the tips of his fingers again.

"What on Earth is this?" he teased and delicately dragged his finger along the bottom of my foot. I laughed and squirmed away from the sensation, nearly falling off the couch. "I had no idea you were so ticklish."

"I am, so stop it." I threw a pillow at him, but he deflected it.

Our pizza box lay devastated on the coffee table. The remaining crusts of the downed wedges littered it, along with an excess of olives I had picked off my pieces. The night had been rather pleasant. Dinner and a movie. It was as close to a date as I'd been in years. All was well, until Dane generously gave me a foot massage, one that had resulted in revealing my Achilles' heel.

He smirked at me across the couch, as he no doubt plotted the many ways he could take advantage of this weakness. He lifted my foot a little higher, and I tensed for a barrage of wiggling fingers. Instead, he leaned forward and licked his tongue along the bottom of my foot. I held still for it, if only out of shock.

When he was done, I laughed at him. "You do know I'm not the best housekeeper. These floors are probably filthy."

He chuckled and looked around at my so-called filthy floors. "You're right. I shouldn't be putting my tongue anywhere near your feet." He glanced down at the part in my robe brought on by my raised foot. I gasped at the inadvertent striptease I was offering and shoved my robe down to cover my lower half. For a moment, he just stared at me, a small smirk of satisfaction propped on his face.

I rolled over and looked back at the television, refusing to give in to the moment. He shifted closer to me, lifting my legs so he could slip underneath them. "Don't," I warned. "I'm enjoying the movie."

"So am I." He rested his hand on my leg and stared at the television hanging above my fireplace.

"Dane," I objected quietly.

"Could you quiet down? I can't hear the movie." His hand shifted up my leg, grazing the skin as it glided under my robe.

"Dane," I said a little more firmly.

"Shhh. I can't hear." He continued to trespass his fingers between my legs, all the while pretending to watch the movie. I gave up trying to control the situation and gave in to his invasive massage. My breath hitched, and he pushed his fingers into me, deepening the experience. I moaned, and Dane shushed me again, insistent that I was interrupting his favorite part.

Despite his request, his ministrations were making it impossible for me to stay quiet. I writhed on the couch beside him, panting and groaning, until he finally eased my yearnings.

He released his grip on me and rested his hand on my leg again. I stared at him, waiting for him to reposition for his own pleasures, but he continued to watch the movie, outright ignoring me. Annoyed by his indifference, I sat up and repositioned so I was straddling him. I thought perhaps this was his intention—to draw me in—but he seemed legitimately surprised by my insistence to include him.

I lifted his shirt over his head and bit my lip as I observed his fine form. There was something about him that seemed sculpted. Not only his muscles, but the very nature of his skin. The smooth untarnished flesh.

He shifted his pants down, allowing me access to yet another sculpted portion of him. Inspired by the perfection below his waistline, I moved down to the floor and stared up at him. "Do you still want to watch TV?" I asked.

He smiled at me. "No."

I drew him into my mouth. He groaned and dropped his head back. "Oh, Hennie, I love you," he drawled. The statement gave me pause, but I was fairly certain he hadn't actually meant to profess his love for *me* so much as my mouth.

Five minutes later, and with no foreseeable end in sight, I gave my neck a break and put my legs to work in his lap. He eagerly accepted the changeover and helped me into position onto him.

Since Dane was one of those special men who took forever to reach his climax, I exhausted myself more than once trying to make a dent in his stubborn appetite. After my third helping, I relaxed and opened my eyes. He looked back at me through hooded, pleasure-filled eyes. I frowned and shook my head at him. "Do you have to watch me?" I panted.

"That's my favorite part." He shifted, resting his hands on the back of the couch, while I took my breather. The interruptions never seemed to bother him.

"I never know what you're thinking."

"I'm thinking about how beautiful you are." He leaned forward and kissed my lips gently.

I stared at him, trying to accept the innocent intimacy. "Do you ever think about hurting me?"

He closed his eyes and clenched his jaw. "Why must you ask me that over and over again?" he whispered, barely in control of the anger he was hiding.

"Because you frighten me," I admitted.

"I frighten you?" He opened his eyes and raised his brow. "You harbor the power of hell and *I* frighten *you*?"

"Yes."

He lowered his brow and moved his hands over to my hips. "Even here? Even in my most vulnerable state, you don't trust me?"

"I want to. So much."

"I am so careful with you, in these moments. You want to know what I think when I'm watching you? I'm thinking how much I want to flip you over and fuck you as hard as I want," he revealed with a sinister intent lurking in his eyes. He leaned forward and wrapped his arms around my back, hugging me a little closer to him. "I don't do that, because I don't want to scare you off. You're the only joy in my life right now, and I will do anything it takes to keep you."

There was a fine line between a romantic declaration of love and a threat of possession. It was all entirely dependent on the receiver's interpretation. Ultimately, how they felt in return was going to be the deciding factor. As I stared down at Dane, I couldn't quite decide where my heart would land. "Did you mean what you said before? Do you... love me?"

Although he seemed loath to admit it, he nodded. "Yes, Hennie, I love you. Don't ask me to explain it. I just do."

"I don't know if I can return those feelings... yet."

"That doesn't matter to me. All I ask is that you let me be near you, to protect you."

"Okay."

He raised his brow, as if stunned by my agreement. I was a little surprised myself, but then again, Dane may well have been the only person left in my life to love me. I couldn't very well throw that away.

"Let's go upstairs."

CHAPTER 5

I BRACED MYSELF AGAINST my headboard, and Dane did the same as he hammered himself into me. It took a moment to acclimate to the barrage of fast-paced pleasure, but as soon as I did, I was roaring my sweet release beneath him.

He panted above me, continuing his enduring pace for several more seconds before his face contorted and he cried out. He collapsed on top of me, pressing me down onto the bed. I pushed up on his shoulders and he released some of his weight to look at me. "Are you okay?"

I smiled. "You didn't break my vagina, if that's what you're asking."

He chuckled. "No, I suppose not. I've wanted to do that for a very long time." He kissed my forehead and then my lips before rolling off me. We both lay there, staring at the ceiling for a moment. "Would you mind if I slept here tonight?"

"No, that's fine."

"Good." I could hear his sigh of relief, as if he'd just proposed marriage and hadn't been rejected.

"I'm going to go wash up. I'll be right back." I slipped out of bed, picked up my robe, and headed to the bathroom.

I jumped in the shower for the second time that night and rinsed myself off. I heard the door open and shut and I waited for Dane to join me in the shower. When he didn't, I peeked out to see what was keeping him.

I stared into the eyes of the last woman I ever wanted to see standing in my bathroom. "Paula." I glared at her. She was still donning her nun's robe—a sacrilege that couldn't be understated, since she was essentially the devil in human form. The only addition to her uniform was that she was sopping wet.

"Hello, Hennie." She smiled at me as she fiddled with the beaded rosary hanging from her waist.

"What the hell do you want?" I shut off the water and climbed out of the tub. "And why are you wet?" I asked as I slipped my fuzzy black robe back on. "Never mind, I don't want to know."

"Just coming to check up on you. I have a job for you."

"Yeah, yeah, he already told me about the molesting father."

"Oh, no, not that. We'll get to that later. I've come across a snag in one of my underground operations."

"Operations?"

"Yes, let's just call them the mob. It got a little out of sorts lately, which normally I wouldn't mind, but dammit if that free will is preventing me from keeping them on track."

"You have a vested interest in the mob's agenda."

"I have a vested interest in the demise of the human species. For the last ten years, I've been running this operation, but for some reason, they've decided to choose a new figurehead. As you might imagine, I was not pleased with their choice."

"You've been running the mob?"

"I have a life beyond you, you know."

"What do you need me to do?"

"Kill them," Paula said flatly.

"Kill them?"

"Yes, all of them."

"But they didn't do anything," I said. She perked a brow at me. "These men are participating in criminal activities. It's against the law, but in terms of morality they don't deserve death. They deserve a jail sentence."

"That's hardly a concern of yours."

"It's a concern of mine when you're asking me to do the killing. I told you from the very beginning, I won't kill innocent people."

"They're hardly innocent." Paula scoffed. "They've killed dozens of men."

"All of whom have probably tried to kill them. This is a gang war, nothing more."

"It's definitely something more. And since I can't kill humans, I need to use you."

"No."

"No?" Her eyes widened, and she stepped forward, pressing me into the wall. "Am I mistaken about what the agreement is here? Your precious nuns get to continue to use my power for the good of all mankind, and I get to use you for my purposes. Isn't that right? Or would you prefer we negotiate on all the good deeds your coven has done up to this point? I wonder how many cancers they've cured. How many little children they've saved? Do you really want to undo all of that for a bunch of no-name mobsters?"

"I know what you are trying to do, Paula. You're planning to turn me into you. Make me as evil and conniving as you."

"Plan?" Paula threw her head back and laughed. "Do you really think this was part of my plans, Hennie? Nobody, not even God himself, intended for you to exist. You are an aberration of nature, born out of pure stubbornness and spite. Look at yourself." She stepped to one side so I could see myself in the mirror. "Your human body is rejecting you."

"It's rejecting the power you keep making me use."

"It's rejecting *you* because you are not compatible with it. You've seen the damage a demon can do to a human body when it possesses it. Imagine what a fallen angel can do to it. God may have given you permission to stay in there, but that doesn't mean you won't eventually kill it by doing so." Paula looked into the mirror, smirking at me through the reflection. "You're a walking corpse, Hennie. You just haven't had the good sense to bury yourself."

I stared blankly at her, knowing she was being truthful, and yet I was still denying it. I could control it. I could keep myself here on Earth. I just needed to stop using the power.

"I'm not going to help you kill your associates."

"You don't necessarily have to kill them. In fact, I'll need some of them alive to continue my work. You can decide, of course. Lady's choice."

"No."

"Oh, you dear, sweet, stupid girl." Paula came closer and touched my cheek gently. "Must I threaten you again?"

"I am protected now. The beast cannot hurt me."

"He can't kill you, but he can still hurt you." She lifted her hand and slapped me across the face. The stinging aftermath was more than the impact. I could smell burned flesh. "And so can I."

Losing the grip on my mature defiance, I spit in her face. She wiped it away and grabbed my chin. Her long taloned nailed pinched into my already burning cheek, making me whimper. Her face bore down on me, eyes with wide oblong slits glared out at me. Even her jaw shifted to one side as if she were chewing cud. I was certain if I ripped away her veil, I would see two rutted horns growing out of her forehead.

"You will do as I command!" her voice grated against my ears.

I felt my will cave, but before I could agree, the door to the bathroom slammed open and Dane stormed in. He barreled into Paula, forcing her back onto the toilet. He stood in front of me stark naked, chest heaving, and eyes boring a hole into my former sister. Despite the terror his anger inspired, it strangely drew me in—a fetish I couldn't control, much like my other addictions.

"Get out," Dane said with measured volume.

"This has nothing to do with you, Hatchet." Paula pushed herself off the toilet to face him.

"Touch her again and I will end you." Dane took a step forward, and to my surprise, Paula backed away. I wasn't sure he was capable of truly killing her, but I suspected he could temporarily banish her from her human form, a feat I hadn't thought possible for any mortal being.

"Be careful how you handle me now, killer. I'm not likely to forget your trespasses when we meet in hell."

Dane grabbed her robe and pulled her back to him. "That's the thing about killers, Sister. We don't tend to think much beyond the moment. Future threats won't work on me."

"Enough." The smooth, calm voice stemmed from the reflection of the man in the mirror. He was standing right beside me, hand on my shoulder, but I hadn't really felt him until I saw his reflection in the mirror.

Dane turned back, looking directly at the face I couldn't see without a reflective surface. To me, he was only a shadow. Or rather, I was a shadow to him, but that was too inexplicable for my brain to accept.

"Let's not pretend this is a game you can win." My shadow squeezed my shoulder. Not painfully, but enough to draw Dane's eyes on the contact. "This body may belong to you, but what is inside is mine. We can bicker and fight until each of us is bloodied or dead, but in the end, you are protecting a vessel." His arms slid around my waist and across my chest with a lateral undulation that didn't match his human form. "A vessel that only needs to be broken for me to attain what's inside."

Dane dropped Paula's robe and approached my serpentine shadow. His nostrils flared as he faced him down, a certain territorial instinct setting in. He didn't bother telling him to release me. He just grabbed his neck and clamped down hard on his voice box to stifle his rhetoric. Not only could he see the face that no one else could, he could touch it, too.

My shadow held tight to his bravado, even as his face turned red. I also did my best to hide the pain Dane's pressure was putting me under. I couldn't breathe and I was certain I would pass out long before my shadow felt the threat of Dane's strength.

I had never understood the connection between us. Why did I share his pain and he mine? I presumed it was because I was a rogue branch of the trinity. The ram and the lion were autonomous extensions, whereas I was still meant to be a part of him. Though we resided in very different worlds, we were effectively still one being.

Paula laughed from her barricaded position in the back of the bathroom. "When will you ever understand this, you simpleton? You're killing the very person you are trying to protect."

Dane examined me, his mouth frowning at the sight of my blue lips and languid eyes. He dropped his grip on my shadow and I took in a much-needed inhalation. Rather than console me, Dane turned away, bracing himself on the counter to take in his own soothing breaths. I knew from experience he found my pain to be especially troubling to his stomach, even if he wasn't the one to inflict it.

"There, there, Dane." My shadow squeezed me close, giving me the creeps with his sinuous phantom touch. "Don't get all bent out of shape. I know this is a confusing concept for you to accept. Let's make it simple for you." Dane looked up at the mirror, narrowing his eyes on him. "Just remember every time you touch this beautiful body..." My shadow raised his hand and dragged a finger down my chest. As much as I wanted to pull away, the grip he had on me was not a physical force that I could slough off. "...you are touching me." He leaned his head close to me and whispered into my ear. "And every time she touches you..." He licked my face with a forked tongue before turning back to Dane's reflection. "...that's me, touching you."

Dane bared his teeth and roared. He turned back to us, fist swinging. I cringed and yelped as it blew past my ear. The drywall beside me erupted into shattered pieces and dust. When he withdrew his attack, I could see my shadow was gone. Only his creepy touch remained, lingering on my skin like the feel of crawling spiders long after I brushed the cobwebs away. I wasn't sure if he had disappeared before or after Dane's fist had landed, but I wasn't about to ask whether my lover had almost smashed my skull in. Certainly not while his fist was still shaking.

I glanced toward Paula, but she was also gone. All that remained of her presence was a card on the toilet. I picked it up and found an address and a time—an appointment I didn't dare miss.

Chapter 6

I CHUCKLED AT THE nonsensical chatter spewing out of the mouth of the man across the table from me. He was an absolute ass, and brazenly sexist. It was all I could do to keep from shoving my stiletto heel into his crotch. As it was, I could already feel the tendrils of hell crawling up my back.

Now, now. No reason to kill a man just for being a dick.

On the other hand, I had reason to believe he was a murderer.

The rationale behind me killing murderers had long since boiled down to the eye-for-an-eye theory. Hardly civilized, and so hypocritical that it became ironic, but ultimately I decided I was reducing the population of homicidal maniacs.

Like I had room to talk on that subject. Since I had been under the assignment of my current trinity of employers, I had killed eight people, maimed six others, and quite possibly driven three mad.

That made me no better than Dane. Actually, it made me worse. At least Dane now felt guilt for his acts of violence. Not me. The eight people I had killed were actively raping, molesting, or abusing others. Short of videotaping them in the act and turning it in to the police, they wouldn't stop what they were doing. Not for long, anyway. Their death was the only solution to stop them.

The ones I had maimed were considered by my shadow to be "acceptable damages." I never bothered to ask what that meant.

The three I drove crazy. Well, that was just a warning, and I was the messenger.

I couldn't imagine the workload I was taking off Paula.

I felt a shoe-less foot slide up my calf. I returned my attention to the man across from me. He was simpering, like he was the cleverest man in the world. As if our meal hadn't been distasteful enough with endless innuendos and sly lip-licking, now I had to contend with his raunchy socks touching my legs.

"Mr. Guitero—"

"Call me Tony," he drawled.

"Tony," I whispered as I leaned forward. "I think there has been some sort of misunderstanding."

"How is that?"

"Well, for one, I'm not a hooker." I kicked my leg forward, tossing his foot off me. He frowned and sat up taller. "Two, I didn't come here to be schmoozed. I came to speak to you on behalf of your ousted figurehead."

"Paul?"

I paused at the masculine designation, but went with it. "Yes. It seems you no longer wish to be represented by... him."

Tony chuckled and looked around. "This must be a joke?" He maneuvered his leg around under the table until his foot was in his shoe again. "Paul wasn't kicked out of our organization." He stood up and tossed his cloth napkin on the table.

"Is that so? Well, he tells a different story. He said you voted him out at the last meeting."

Tony paused and stared at me. "So, Paul kept you in the loop on our meetings." He looked me over and then scratched his head. "How much did he tell you?"

"Let's not get into details here. I happen to know you're planning to have a meeting later tonight. That's why I'm here. You're my in-guy. So be a good little man and pay the check, so we can zip downstairs to check on the laundry."

Tony checked his watch and pulled a long wallet from his suit jacket pocket. He laid a few c-notes on the table and motioned for me to accompany him. Outside of the restaurant, he guided the way through the hotel lobby to the elevators. Once inside, he typed in a code and pressed the button for the basement.

I leaned back against the wall and waited. Tony turned his head slightly to speak to me. "You know they won't be here for another hour."

"I know, but I wasn't exactly interested in how you wanted to spend that hour."

He let out a huff and raised his chin. "Your loss, bitch."

We stepped out of the elevator onto the basement floor and meandered our way into the core of the hotel's laundry facility. I instantly felt the hot humidity of the dryers, and the smell of detergents overwhelmed my nostrils. It was a smart place to conduct seedy business. The rumble of washing machines covered their voices. And in the case of irreparable differences, there was plenty of bleach to clean up the mess.

Tony stopped in an alley of over-sized washing machines. He leaned against a stainless-steel table, which was no doubt used for sorting by the hard-working hotel staff. "What did Paul tell you about us?"

"Don't worry about that. I'm not here to stick my nose in your business. I'm just here to remind you that Paul isn't the type of... person you want to mess with."

"Is that so?" He eyed me carefully, as if he still couldn't believe I was there. As if the audacity of a woman demanding his compliance was new to him, making me far more interesting than annoying. "Are you and Paul a couple?"

I snorted and shook my head. "'Fraid not. He's not quite my taste." Not to mention that any relationship between Paul and me would have to be defined as autoeroticism.

"So this isn't about some lover's revenge?" He moved over to me, leaning on the washer beside me. I shook my head. "I don't get it then."

I smiled and shook my head. "Trust me, you will. I just don't want to get into the big show until the rest of your crew arrives. It kind of helps to keep me focused on one task at a time."

"You sound a lot like Paul." Tony waggled his finger at me. "He was always alluding to his endgame. Threatening us without actually doing anything. I mean, don't get me wrong, Paul was super scary, but after six years of bullshit, I couldn't take it anymore. Evil glares have an expiration date, and talk is cheap if you're not willing to get your hands dirty.

"Now me?" Tony pressed his hand to his chest. "I'm willing to get my hands dirty. I'm willing to do what it takes to get the power and keep the power." He grinned. "That's why I killed Paul."

I dipped my brow at him. Either I was making too many assumptions and Paul was not Paula, or Tony had actually tried to kill the incarnation of the devil. No wonder Paula was pissed. "You killed Paul."

"Yes, and I took his seat as the leader of our little organization, a position I have been coveting for quite some time."

"Ooh, coveting, that's number ten. That's like a gateway drug for up-and-coming assholes."

Tony narrowed his eyes at me. "I don't get you. You come here unarmed, shooting off your mouth like you own the joint, and just like Paul, you got nothing to back it up. How did you think this would end?"

"I know how it will end." I frowned.

"So do I." Tony grabbed my shoulder and yanked me forward, even as he opened the door to the washer beside him. My face collided with plastic and metal. Stars blocked my vision for a moment and I hit the floor.

I could feel Tony's arms around me, and I kicked at his legs with my heels. He lifted me up, reducing my leverage to how deep my nails could dig into his arms. My head took another hit, and I landed on something hard and cold. I kicked at Tony's hands as they pushed on me, putting me deeper into the darkness. The stars cleared, and I instantly realized where I was.

I looked back in time to see the porthole door of the washer close on me. I pushed on the window, but I could already hear the mechanical click of the locking mechanism. I banged on the door.

"Let me out of here!" I screamed to be heard through the double-layered plastic.

Tony leaned down, bringing his face in line with mine. "I bet my first offer isn't sounding so disgusting to you now."

"Don't make me gag."

He gritted his teeth, but continued to smile. "Like I said, your loss, bitch."

Water poured into the machine. "Don't do this, Tony. You've already pissed off one of us, don't add a second."

"And why is that?"

"Because you won't like who they send after me. Not one bit."

Tony chuckled. "There it is." He poked the glass. "That potential for danger, and yet here I am... killing you!" He laughed and walked away.

The washer rocked, gaining the momentum to roll its heavy load over and over again. I braced my hands on the drum and took the roll like a trooper. However, the three subsequent rolls had me ready to vomit. I sputtered away the water as it splashed over me, breathing when I had the opportunity. Unfortunately, the danger I was facing wasn't drowning. It was suffocation. The drum was large, but it was watertight, which meant it was airtight too. Between the waning oxygen and a dizzying ride, I would eventually pass out. I supposed drowning would technically be the cause of death.

Not unless I could use my power like the supervillain I truly was.

That was the kicker of this whole arrangement, though. My shadow was the one divvying out my power supply. I had been on his leash from day one. He had control of the magical flow. If he didn't agree with my usage, he could yank it away at any moment.

The question was, did he want me to use it to save myself? After all, his ultimate goal had always been to get me back. What better way than to let me get myself killed?

I tapped into the dark core inside of me, strumming the kinetic ball, begging it to release itself to me, but it wouldn't budge. I felt a little of it release, but not enough to save myself.

I coughed up a badly timed breath and looked toward the washer window. I had expected to see his reflection there, taunting me, but he wasn't around.

"Oh, fine." I spoke aloud. "Just when I need you." I laughed and spit out a dose of water. "I don't know why I thought you would help me. You hate me, after all. That's the real reason I left you, wasn't it? I'm the part of yourself you can't stand! The part that actually gives a damn about something. The only part of you that isn't an evil fuck. Well, guess what? I'm coming right back to you. I'm gonna die in a goddamn washing machine and then I'll be by your side, making you feel guilty for all the shit you've put people through. Is that really what you want?"

The washing machine clunked to a stop, and the water settled at my back before draining away. I blinked away the water in my eyes. A figure moved around outside of my death trap, pushing buttons and tugging on the door. After a loud click, the door released and hands reached in for me.

I looked up at Dane's furious eyes as he yanked me through the porthole and laid me on the stainless-steel table behind him. He embraced my face with his hands, checking that I was conscious. "Are you okay?"

"Yes," I whispered.

"Good." He released me and walked away. I tipped my head back and watched him leave. No goodbye. No long-stated expression of his relief—just "good" and gone.

He was angry.

Really angry.

CHAPTER 7

I FOUND MY HIGH heels and ran after Dane. He had taken the stairs up since that was likely the way he got down there without a code. I took the elevator up, but I hadn't gained the time I was hoping to. "Dane!" I called to him as he reached the automatic doors at the front entrance of the hotel. He didn't even flinch at hearing his name.

I realized a bit late that my water-logged dress and hair were drawing more attention than Dane's identity could afford. I slowed my racing steps to a natural speed and pushed my hair from my face.

When I reached the sidewalk outside, there was no one in sight, including Dane. I sighed and crossed my arms. Maybe that was for the best. I knew why he was mad. I had left him again. Slipped out of the house without telling him where I was going or why. Little did I know this was the one occasion I actually could have used backup.

I looked at the clock in the hotel lobby. I still had some time before the official mob meeting. Just enough time to get some new clothes. I yanked my car key from out of my bra where it had miraculously stayed throughout my rinse cycle.

A few minutes later, I walked into a downtown boutique, sopping wet, makeup smeared, and turning a little purple from my tumble. Several of the shoppers took notice of me. One of the salesgirls approached me at the door and asked, "Is there anything I can help you with?" No doubt asking the question on several more levels than simply fashion.

"I need a new outfit."

"Have anything in mind?"

"Something dry." I winked at her and she smiled. "But also, something that screams *you fucked with the wrong woman*."

The salesgirl lost her congenial grin, but the smirk of a woman familiar with life's irritations quickly replaced it. "I have just the thing."

Just the thing indeed.

Before long Megan had brought me a towel, a small stack of makeup from their in-house line, and a selection of business suits that trespassed between *I am woman, hear me roar* and *I am woman—therefore I look really hot in this outfit*. By the time she finished with me, I was going to look like the CEO of a Fortune 500 company. Appropriate, since I was probably going to contribute $500 to her commission.

I slipped into the dressing room and slid the curtain shut. I shrugged off my little black dress, now tight as a rubber suit. I got it over my hips and onto the floor when the rings of the curtain door scraped open. I gasped and covered myself, despite having adequate bikini coverage with my bra and panties.

I looked up at Dane's perplexed face. "What are you doing?" we both said simultaneously.

He pushed into the tiny space and closed the curtain on us. "Why are you shopping?" he whispered. "You almost just died."

"I am not entirely sure why you think those two activities wouldn't go perfectly well together."

He stared at me, depositing my joke under the category of "things *she* thinks are funny" in his mind.

"What are you doing here? I thought you left." I used the towel to blot off my skin before working on my hair.

"I was waiting. Why aren't you going home?" He picked up one of the suits the salesgirl had picked out for me. "Are you seriously going back in there?"

"I don't really have a choice."

"Yes, you do, Hennie. You just refuse to give up your link to his power."

"Oh, this has nothing to do with him anymore. That asshole tried to murder me. Now it's personal."

"Would you listen to yourself? You'll use any excuse to use it. I don't know if you noticed it or not, but your power wasn't doing you any good inside of that washer."

"I know."

"He doesn't care if you live or die."

"I know."

"I do."

He was still angry, but the reason for it was a little clearer to me. He was worried about me. He was disappointed and irritated by my stupidity, but he was ultimately concerned that I had almost died. That he might not have been there to save me, because I keep pushing him away, or outright running away from him.

"Thank you for saving me."

"What if I wasn't there? What if that man had a gun?"

"I know, I'm sorry."

"You have to stop leaving me behind."

"I know."

Dane grabbed my shoulders. "Not, *I know*! I *will*! You have to let me in, Hennie. Whether you are prepared to love me or not, I am the only one that can protect you from him, and them." He nodded toward the figurative bad guys. "And yourself."

My mouth opened and he tensed, pressing on my arms a little tighter.

"Miss," the salesgirl called in. "How are those working for you?"

"Um, I haven't tried them yet. I'm going to dry out a bit first, if that's okay."

"Sure, take your time. I have scissors out here for the tags if you want to wear them out."

"Thanks."

I heard her footsteps move away, and I turned my attention back to Dane. He was starting to give up. The glow in his eyes was dimming and his hands were sliding down my arms.

"Okay," I whispered.

His brow dipped, and he shook his head. "I mean it, Hennie. This isn't a joke."

I sighed and tossed my head back. "I won't lie to you about where I'm going anymore. I won't leave you behind."

"You promise?"

"Yes, I promise."

Dane relaxed and pulled me into a hug. It felt strange. I wasn't sure we had ever hugged before, at least not outside of a sexual encounter.

I let my hands drift up to his back, pressing gently on him. He turned his head to speak into my ear. "You still don't trust me, do you?"

"Are you still hunting me?"

"I don't have to hunt you if you stop running away." His fingers traced down my spine, pausing at my underwear line. "Are you really done running from me?" He kissed my neck, dragging his tongue as he moved to the next piece of skin.

"Dane, I have to get back soon."

"Sounds like you're getting ready to run."

"No, I just don't want to miss them. I don't know how long the meeting will go."

Dane pushed me up against the brick wall behind me. He held me there, palm pressing between my breasts. "What do you want more, Hennie? Me or your power high?"

I stared back at him, not daring to tell him the truth. Not that I didn't enjoy my sex life, but there was no competition for what hell offered. After all, the devil was a professional tempter. "I want you," I lied.

Dane moved his hand over to my breast. He leaned in and kissed me, removing my underwear with his free hand. The jangle of his belt signaled that he had freed himself as well.

His hands moved beneath me, cradling my butt. He lifted me and entered me, pressing me against the wall. His maddening pace was enough to bring me to a fast close. I bit his shoulder to keep myself from groaning too loudly. He, in turn, shuddered and grunted quietly in my ear.

He released my legs, and for a moment, we leaned on each other and the wall. I looked up at him, admiring the way he looked at me—carnally and yet with a certain tenderness that hinted at his previous profession of love. He touched my cheek and kissed my lips. "Time to get dressed. We have work to do."

CHAPTER 8

R ED WAS ALWAYS THE best color for the devil. That's why I chose the red pantsuit with a fitted blazer and wide-legged pants. I pulled my hair back into a high, tight ponytail and put on enough eyeliner to make a raccoon look twice.

When I finally stepped back onto the basement floor, the power I was so familiar with was tickling at my palms and pressing at my back. Although Dane was eager to accompany me this time around, he stayed at my back, allowing me to take the lead.

The members of the crime syndicate were just around the corner, bickering about money, or guns. The click of my heels might have signaled my arrival, but the noise from the washers masked the sound in the basement. No doubt an intentional step to prevent anyone from overhearing their conversation.

I rounded the corner and looked over the cluster of eight men around the stainless-steel table. Tony Guitero was at the far end, sitting in a chair, with his hands tented over his lap. His eyes widened as he took in my face. My still breathing face. He stood from his chair, drawing the attention of the other members. They each in turn looked back at me, frowning at my presence.

"Who the fuck is this?" one of them asked.

"Oh, don't mind me, boys. Continue with your diabolical plans." I pulled a folding chair over from the corner and placed it on the opposite end of the table to Tony. I swept it off with my hand and sat primly on it, crossing my legs at the knee. "Hello, Tony." I smiled down at his snarling face.

"How the fuck did you get out of there?"

"You didn't think I had come alone, did you?"

Dane stepped out from the shadows behind me, letting each of the men get a good look at him.

"Hey, I know you," one of the men said to him.

"Do you?" Dane asked, staring him down virulently.

He frowned and shook his head. "Nah, I guess I was wrong." They each kept a watchful eye on the other.

"You might have a guard dog, but I have three." Tony snapped his fingers and three men came out from behind the row of hanging uniforms behind him. They drew their guns and aimed them at me. Tony leaned over the table and waggled his head. "Now, what were you saying to me earlier? Something about teaching us all a lesson?"

I smiled and looked down at my hands, folded neatly in my lap. The nails had taken on a purple hue, as if the skin beneath was bruising. Just another piece of proof that the power I was using was not compatible with my humanity. Not that it would stop me from using it.

I felt the familiar tingle at the tips of my fingers. The power coursing through me was waiting to be designated and directed. I had seen it once—the repercussions of a physical defense, anyway. It was just a quiver in the air, an echo of an invisible force propelling away from my body.

What could I do with this magnificent power residing inside of me?

Anything.

Anything. The word whispered in the back of my mind, but I ignored it.

"Easy, boys." I raised my hands slowly in surrender. "There's no reason to get into a *heated* situation."

The men shifted the grip on their weapons until they had no choice but to drop them. The weapons clanged against the concrete, drawing everyone's eyes. Tony looked at his men, baffled. "Are you daft? Pick up your guns." One of the men bravely reached for his revolver, but his skin sizzled on contact.

Tony turned his attention back to me, brow dipped deep into his eyes.

"Well, you said you were getting tired of all the talk. I thought you would want a show this time."

"Who the fuck *is* this?" the same man as before asked.

"I represent your former boss," I said.

"What is this, Tony? I thought you took care of Paul."

"I did," Tony ground out. "He is at the bottom of the river. Which is exactly where this bitch is about to be." Tony pulled his own gun from under his jacket.

There was no ceremony in his execution. Just the rise of the gun and the twitch of his trigger finger. However, the natural progression of time slowed to a crawl so I could see the threat advancing on me. The air in front of the gun's barrel bloomed into a tiny cloud of smoke, before erupting in light. The bullet aimed at my forehead appeared, surrounded by a ring of fire.

The dull roar of the chamber explosion reverberated through the basement. The bullet propelled forward with a plume of fire at its back. For a moment, I watched the expanding light, playing chicken with the bullet. When it was almost close enough to touch, I released my defense, which, by any definition, was still an offense.

The power rippling off me impacted the bullet like a tsunami to a boat. The metal cylinder shattered like glass. The splinters of metal scattered, hitting the two men closest to my end of the table.

I was barely back in real time before Dane's body jumped in front of me, practically lying on my lap. I looked at his sideways position, truly bewildered by his impromptu hug. It wasn't until I saw the look on his face that I understood he'd intended to sacrifice himself for me.

I should have been touched.

At the very least, his fast action should have impressed me. He might have actually saved me, if I hadn't already saved myself. That, of course, would have meant he would be dead instead of me.

I should have felt something.

Something other than irritation for him interrupting my super cool badass performance. All I could think was that I shouldn't have brought him. He was cramping my style.

Dane realized his heroics were unnecessary and lifted himself off me. The men to my left and right moaned about the shrapnel in their faces while the two next to them tried to figure out what had just happened. Tony, on the other hand, seemed to understand completely. His eyes were wide and fearful. Strangely, though, they weren't actually on me.

"I killed you," he whispered, his gun hand shaking slightly as he shifted his aim away from me.

I turned to see who he was looking at. Behind me, hidden in the shadows of an excess of pipes, I could see a figure, the head tucked down, and for a moment the flare of a lighter lit the face.

At first glimpse, I thought it was Paula. And yet, it was not her at all.

The cherry of a cigarette glowed brightly, followed by a puff of smoke that seemed to absorb back into the designer suit as it emerged into the light. The footfalls of high-sheen loafers matched the heavy thump of my heart as I looked at the face of *Paul*.

I had always thought Paula was an especially attractive woman, but now in the masculine form, she was alluring in an entirely new way. Or perhaps it wasn't new.

The tousled charcoal hair and olive skin. Pale green eyes buoyed by thick lashes. That perfectly trimmed goatee. This was the man haunting my reflection and trespassing in my dreams.

Was it really him all along? Or was she him? Did it even matter if they were all the same? Man, woman, or beast, it was still one-third of hell's trinity. Serpent, ram, and lion. Mind, body, and spirit.

They were interchangeable; I supposed. It was all a matter of who was needed. Paula's physical form could manifest as anyone. I presumed she kept the same form to avoid confusion. However, now staring at the flesh and blood male version of her, I realized we had already met. I just hadn't known it at the time.

Paul stopped next to me, turning his head in a wide arch to look down on me. A shiver ran down my spine as I stared back at him, mouth draped open. My feelings were a mixture of fear and excitement. The first time I had seen him, I had been too distracted by the pain of a stab wound to truly appreciate the primal urges his perfection called to. I was certain it was his angelic side and not his evil that I was connecting with.

At least, I hoped it was.

Paul took a drag of his cigarette, keeping a cool gaze on me. He blew out the smoke, which once again wrapped around his body, before disappearing into his Armani fabric. "I take it they haven't been behaving." He spoke with the same dulcet tone of my shadow. He turned to offer Tony a cool reception. "Have you, Tony?"

"No, no! This is impossible. I strangled you with my bare hands. I watched you die."

"You saw what I wanted you to see."

"I watched your body sink to the bottom of the river."

Paul smoothed down his beard and shrugged. "What can I say? I'm hard to kill."

"What do you want?" Tony renewed the aim of his gun.

Paul's eyes seemed to glow at the prospect of answering that question. His mouth curved slightly. "Revenge."

I felt a wave of anger stir inside of me, as if I were the one wanting revenge. I didn't question where it was coming from, or how it had overtaken me so fast. I just opened the floodgates and unleashed the hell within.

CHAPTER 9

I SCREAMED AND WRITHED in pain on the floor of the basement. I could smell something burning, like chicken feathers, only much worse. I coughed on the rank smell and the smoke that accompanied it.

"Let it go!" Dane yelled at me, trying to lift me or turn me.

I pushed him away. Everything was a blur. All I could remember was the hatred pouring through my veins, adding to the intensity of my power high.

I opened my eyes and saw glossy loafers in front of me. I looked up at Paul's face, my shadow, my daydream, my nightmare, and the mind that I belonged to. It wasn't a fantasy of intimate possession. It was a fact of my existence. *I was his.*

Paul looked down at me, a slight frown on his face. "You should do as he says, Hennie."

"Do what?" I groaned.

"Let go of the rosary beads!" Dane yelled in my ear.

I looked down at the black beads I had wrapped around my hand, clenched in my fist. I always kept them close to me when I used my power—a measuring device to check my degree of evil, before and after I performed my fiendish tasks.

The tiny necklace had burned my skin, causing it to bleed. Even the blood sizzled as it hit the rosary. The pain I was feeling was excruciating, and it didn't seem possible that such a small thing could cause it, but when Dane finally ripped the beads away from me, the agony subsided.

The broken string hurled the little plastic beads everywhere. I watched them all go, bouncing and rolling. The farther away they got, the better I felt.

I looked back up at the devil before me. "What did you do to me? What was that?"

Paul shook his head. "I just gave you a taste of what it's like to be me."

"I already know what it's like to be you. That's why I left you, you son of a bitch!"

"Careful, Hennie. I think your cup runneth over. I wouldn't want you to do anything rash. At least, not again." Paul smiled and sauntered away. Enraged by his dismissal, I jumped to my feet and ran after him.

I nearly reached him to tackle him, but he turned in time to catch me. He braced his hand against my sternum and bowed his head down to speak to me. "You can't fight me." His face and body transformed, along with his clothes. I stared at Paula's face, the more familiar human form. "As much as we want to, Hennie, we can't fight each other. We are the same."

"I am nothing like you!" I screamed at her.

"Is that so? Then what happened back there?" She nodded behind me.

"You made me do this!" I pointed at her.

"No." Paula shook her head somberly. "I only opened you to the anger I felt. That..." Paula pointed behind me. "...is what *you* chose to do with it."

I looked back, but I couldn't see around the washers and dryers. Dane was standing near them, watching our conversation. He wasn't happy about the situation.

I took a step forward, but Dane shifted into my path. "Don't."

"What did I do to them?"

"If you honestly don't remember, let's keep it that way."

"No, I need to know."

He held out his hand. "You need to know, but you don't have to see."

I looked down at my hand. The rosary burn had already healed up. Then why was there still smoke in the air? Why was there still a stench making my eyes water?

I darted around Dane, refusing to let him censor me, like my own mind.

Sitting around the table were nine blackened corpses, plus the three collapsed on the floor behind them, each of them still smoking from the fiery death I had brought down on them. The sunken eyes and exposed teeth did nothing to hide the look of fear on their faces.

I stopped at the end of the table and broke into tears. Not perhaps for the men before me, but rather the realization of my own conscience being crushed by the weight of an addictive satanic power, a power that even the devil himself could barely control, because he was just a little too human.

Too human for heaven. Too angelic for Earth. The only place right for him was hell. A place where anger can survive for an eternity. Where love turns to jealousy and lust. Where power corrupts, and absolute power corrupts absolutely.

Just like it does here on Earth.

CHAPTER 10

I HADN'T KNOWN WHAT to say to Dane on the drive home. I wasn't sure if I owed him an apology. I was certain I owed *someone* an apology. If not Dane or the poor staff at the hotel laundry, I at least owed God an apology.

Sorry I exist.

For the first time since He had bestowed permission on me, I wondered why He'd done it. It couldn't have been for anyone's benefit. I wasn't saving lives. The fact of the matter was, I was endangering lives.

It's not your fault. The words were only a whisper in the back of my mind, but I knew they weren't mine. I had plenty of people rattling around in my head lately, but this voice sounded different to me. Soothing and sweet. I wondered if it was my conscience. Could I have a conscience? Wasn't I already the conscience of the devil? Could the conscience of the devil have a conscience?

It was all too complicated, and I had far too many questions. So I ignored the voice because there was one thing I was very certain of: it was my fault.

When we reached the house, and our silence persisted, I summoned the nerve to speak.

"Dane—"

"Don't," he interrupted as he got out of the passenger side of the vehicle.

I jumped out of the car to follow him. "I'm trying to apologize."

"I know," he called back to me. "So don't."

We reached the front stoop of my house, but I waited to unlock the door. Dane stared back at me, not explaining his statement. "Why won't you let me apologize?"

"Because nothing that happened there tonight affected me."

"Of course it did. I turned into a monster before your very eyes."

Dane's gaze dropped to the cold concrete beneath us and he shook his head. "This is not about monsters and demons. This isn't about good or bad. As far as I'm concerned, those men were bad people, and they deserved to die."

"Yes, but not that way. Not so painfully. Not without any mercy."

"I don't know that, Hennie. And neither do you." Dane looked out into the neighborhood, eyeing the area carefully. His vision was no longer that of a man. He could detect things human eyes could not. I wondered how often he saw the shadows of demons. I wondered how many threats trespassed on us every day that he didn't mention or acknowledge.

"I imagine if you ask the families of the women I have killed how justice would be best served, you might get some varying answers. Answers that would be no more humane than what you have just done. There are moments in everyone's life when they react to their anger or lust or greed. Times when they behave cruelly. I can see those moments in myself and I hate them as much, if not more, than those families. You at least can have pride in knowing you rid the world of hurtful people. I, however, carry the burden of knowing I have hurt the innocent. There was no justice in my murders. There was no logic to my cruelty. I live with the guilt of my actions every single day. Apologies don't change what I have done and they don't heal those I've hurt. Even if I could apologize, there's no one that would listen.

"You could apologize to me—to ease some of your guilt," Dane said. "But I don't want that. I want the guilt of those deaths to stay with you. Much as the guilt of my crimes is always with me. It's the only way you can keep a clear mind. It's the only way you can learn from it."

"What could I possibly learn from tonight, other than how ridiculously easy I can be manipulated?"

Dane raised his hand and pressed it against my cheek. "You have been manipulated this entire time. The fires of hell around you have grown embers to flames and you can't even feel it. He will use you until you are so corrupted that you are nothing more than a lapdog begging at his feet for more power."

"And what, I can't stop it?" I asked as I unlocked the door to the house. I had already considered the scenario he was predicting. What junkie doesn't imagine what they might do to get their next high? Money is disposable. Pride was expendable. At what point did morality become sacrificeable? "What if the draw is too strong and I can't resist him?"

Dane took a deep breath and lowered his hand from my cheek. His eyes turned dark, and he glowered at me. "Don't make me answer that question." He twisted the doorknob and pushed his way into the house. I stood on the porch, gazing out onto the surrounding streets. There were a good number of threats, no doubt lurking in the shadows, waiting for me to let my guard down and invite them in.

Little did I know the biggest threat against me was already inside.

CHAPTER 11

I SLEPT FITFULLY THAT night, ever vigilant of the dangers lurking in my future, including the one sleeping next to me. I told myself there was no reason to fear Dane, but that wasn't true. It never had been.

From the day Dane had converted from a serial killer into our resident demon hunter, he could sense the darkness dripping off me. He had freely admitted his desire to hunt me. I had taken the statement as erotically suggestive, but it was all too clear that his draw to me was not purely sexual. His cravings for murder had transformed into a bloodlust for demonic death. The deeper I trespassed into the pit of hell, the more I would look like the demons he so desired to hunt and kill.

I wondered if that was the plan for him all along.

Had Sister Aggie pointed us to him to protect the coven? Or had she done it to protect the coven from me?

Was he the failsafe?

"Geez, Hennie, you're so dramatic." The voice carried through the room just as something clanked on my vanity.

I bolted upright in bed, prepared to end the stranger in my room, but it wasn't a stranger. "Jess?"

"I mean, I know the whole of hell is knocking on the inside of your skull, but the victim act is so annoying to listen to." Jessica picked up the perfume bottle she had knocked over to give it a sniff. "Eew." She grimaced and threw the bottle in the trash.

I stared at the back of her head, trying to figure out what manner of waking dream I was having. Was it a nightmare or a fantasy? When my eyes shifted to the mirror, I could see her warm eyes staring back at me, her round face smiling slightly as if she was rather pleased she had stunned me into silence.

"Well, aren't you going to say hi?"

"Paula, is that you?" I grimaced, all at once realizing this couldn't be real. "You conniving little bitch."

"Yikes, I guess you two aren't getting along."

"Stop this act," I insisted.

"I'm not Paula."

My eyes narrowed, hearing the truth in her voice.

"I'm Jessica."

Again, the truth.

I shook my head vehemently. "No, that can't be. You're dead."

"So?" She shrugged her shoulders and went back to exploring the arsenal of makeup on my vanity. I turned back to check if Dane was awake, but he was sleeping soundly beside me. "Oh my God, please tell me you are not still using this lipstick. I gave you this like eight years ago." Jess took it upon herself to toss my favorite lipstick into the trash.

"What are you...? How are you...? Oh, Jess..." My voice turned to whisper as I frowned at her face. Though she had died young, she actually looked a little old to me. Still beautiful and without marring of age, but somehow her eyes reflected the wisdom she had gained since leaving me.

Even as I tried to formulate the deep-felt sorrow that was twisting my heart and disrupting my breathing, Jess rolled her eyes and mimicked the sound of the buzzer. "Meeeep!" She twisted around on the short stool and made a farting sound with her tongue. "Pbbbllltttt! I'm sorry the portion of the evening where we go through the emotional bullshit has been cut."

"But you're here. I have so much to tell you. So much I need to say."

"And you're not going to get to say it, because you, my friend, have far more important things to worry about than a cathartic reunion. Besides, this meet-and-greet is only temporary and we can't waste a minute of it. So, first thing first, my bestie..." Jess turned back to face the mirror. "Do you think I should grow my bangs out?"

I clenched my teeth and let out a temperamental growl. Her dismissal irritated me, but I was even more frustrated by her personality. "No, of course you shouldn't grow out your bangs. We've had this conversation a million times. Your bangs are your thing."

"Yes, but I was the last person on Earth to have bangs, and I really want to pull my hair back. See?" Jess pulled her hair back with one hand and combed her bangs back with the other, letting her forehead show completely.

"Then use a barrette. I can't believe we are having this conversation. I can't believe you would come back from the dead to see me and we're going to have the same argument we had for the last ten years. You look cute as shit with bangs, and anyone who tells you otherwise is a liar."

"Fine." Jess let her hair flop back down and moved over to sit on the edge of the bed beside me. "So how are things going with Mr. Hottie?" As if sensing he was being talked about, Dane let out a slight mumble and rolled onto his back. He slept in the nude, but luckily the sheet was covering his strongest attribute. His chest was bare and his legs exposed. "Damn, how the hell did you end up with him?"

"Ouch." I grimaced at her.

"Oh, no, no, no." She waved her hand at me. "I don't mean it like that. You're obviously gorgeous and sexy and smart and I'm assuming good in the sack, but..." Jess's eyes drifted back to the half-naked man beside me. "I'm just super jelly."

"Thanks, I guess." When her eyes didn't readily release from Dane, I cleared my throat. "Jess, do you want to tell me why you're here?"

"Oh, right." Jess snapped out of her fantasy and looked me square in the eye. "You... Need... To..." With a quick shift, she raised her hand and slapped me across the face. The stinging pain resonated skin-deep. "Snap out of it!" Jess yelled at me.

I gaped at her and glanced over at Dane. It was a little disappointing that my dead best friend could just waltz into my bedroom and smack me around while he snored quietly beside me. "What the hell?" I squawked at her.

"The hell is what?" she sniped. "You are sliding down the rabbit hole. Having a happy little trip with the white rabbit, right along with Tweedledee and Tweedledum. Well, I got news for you: this psychedelic suicide mission is over." She waggled her head as she spoke. "I am not going to stand by and watch you destroy what God gave you just because nobody decided to come to your pity party."

"What is that supposed to mean?"

"It means the minute your coven dropped you, you fell into the arms of the enemy."

"Fell into? What are you talking about? He practically owns me."

"Owns you? Please, you can put up as many inspirational posters as you want to, but there is nobody on God's green Earth that can convince you to feel proud, or be confident, or *just do it*." Jess air quoted.

"What are you talking about?"

"I'm talking about the stupid diet books that tell you not to feel guilty if you fall off the program. I'm talking about those big girls who wear bikinis and then tell you to be confident in your body. I'm talking about the fucking bangs!"

"What?"

"Don't you get it, Hennie?"

"No!"

"You can tell yourself to do something, but if that little voice in the back of your head tells you otherwise, then you will never be able to do it. That little voice is so powerful it can take someone strong and willful and turn them weak."

"And what happens if that person is weak to begin with?" I asked. "What happens if she's all alone and scared and guilty and tired?"

"See? This is the pity party I'm talking about!"

"Oh, come on, Jess."

"No, I didn't come here to cheer you up. I didn't come here to give you a shoulder to cry on. I came here to let you know that first of all, you are not alone. You have never been alone. And second of all, you are not weak. You are so strong. You just have to stop letting him control you. You have to start believing in yourself."

"Is that an inspirational poster I hear?"

Jess shook her head slowly. "No, Hennie, you still aren't getting it. You aren't the one who needs the inspirational poster. You are the voice that can dismantle it. You are the voice inside of *his* head. And there is nothing more powerful than that. Fight him." Jess gripped my shoulders and gave them a squeeze, her eyes wide, serious and stern. "Stop playing his game or you will lose. And then we will all lose."

"What do you mean, we will *all* lose?"

"Who are you talking to?" Dane asked beside me.

I turned to find him propped up on his elbows, staring at me. By the time I looked back to Jess, she was gone, the pressure of her hands against my skin still fresh in my mind. "No one," I whispered and fell back against my pillow. All at once, I felt sad, as if Jess had died again. It should have been comforting, knowing that she had my back, that I wasn't alone. But, of course, it didn't feel that way to me. It felt like my friends had abandoned me. Left me alone to...

Holy shit.

Jess was right. I needed to be done with this pity party. Starting now.

CHAPTER 12

"WHAT DO YOU THINK you're doing?" My shadow, the incorporeal Paul, stared back at me through the bathroom mirror. It was as close to a face-to-face conversation as we could ever get.

"What do you think I'm doing?" I said, combing back my hair. After only three days of avoiding my magical powers, I had already noticed the color coming back into my skin. My cheeks were rosy and my skin was becoming a little plumper. I had never been so happy to gain weight in my life. There was certainly nothing sexy about bony ribs and hips.

"I think you're trying to avoid me," he said, stepping up closer to me. He still couldn't touch me, but it didn't mean I couldn't feel the energy coursing through him. Coursing through me. The connection between us. His mere proximity was enough to strum the nerve endings in my body far deeper than a physical touch, alerting me to the potential for pleasure and pain.

"I think you're trying to manipulate me into becoming your uber evil earthbound bitch. And I'm not going to let you do it."

"And why exactly do you think you can stop me?"

"Because it's what I want to do. And whether or not you want me to want to do something else, you don't actually have the power to make me do it."

His eyes glistened with hatred that was usually reserved for Paula's beautiful face. His jaw clenched as he smirked. "And you just all of a sudden decided you no longer need to do what I say?"

"So long as what you want me to do is not what I want to do, then we have nothing to discuss."

He stepped closer. His sinuous arm wrapped around my waist. He brought his face up close to mine and whispered in my ear. "Are you saying you don't want this power anymore?" The energy inside of me bristled, blooming into something abruptly titillating. I huffed and leaned over the counter, bracing myself through each of the penetrating waves that started in my belly and reverberated to my limbs. It was a no-holds-barred temptation. Something that no one would be able to resist and still maintain their sanity. "Are you saying you don't want to be one of us anymore?"

"What I am saying is that I wish to resume the role I've always played in your life. I will continue to be your conscience, your compass, and your only remaining barrier to pure evil." My eyes flapped open, and I stared at him. "Now get your slithering hands off of me."

His eyes glowed with futile anger. He couldn't do anything to retaliate against me. Not without endangering himself. He knew it, and I knew it. But even when I thought he might risk the pain just to teach me a lesson, his anger faded and a small smile perched back on his lips. "So be it." He disappeared between the blinks of my eyes. As pleased as I was to see him go, I couldn't help but wonder what had prompted his immediate change of temperament. And how I might suffer for it.

CHAPTER 13

I YAWNED AND SHIFTED deeper into the couch. Dane was on the opposite side, taking up his half and then some. I had been sharing nicely, but I couldn't get comfortable. Never mind that there was no semblance of order to our overlapping legs. Never mind that Dane was a walking, talking furnace, and just being near him required air conditioning. And never mind that we spent a week cooped up in my house, trying to avoid the police, FBI, and, oh yes, Satan.

The problem was really about his sudden disinterest in sex. He explained the addictive quality of sex. He actually even brought up the Alcoholics Anonymous mantra for avoiding relationships during the first six months of sobering. It was logical, of course. Especially since the devilish power inside of me had been becoming more and more sexualized. As a human, there were a few tried-and-true pleasures that could lure me back time and time again. A straight-out druggy high, though effective in an addiction sense, would draw too much attention to my shadow's goals. You don't start off offering heroin when chocolate cake is all you need.

The part of our little dry spell I didn't understand was why he was so freaking calm. In addition to casually watching television with me, he was casually eating with me. He even showered with me! Nothing! Not a goddamn dribble of drool.

I kicked my foot into the back of his thigh. He jumped and looked around before settling back on me. "What is it?" he asked. He looked genuinely concerned, so I kicked him again. "Hey!" He frowned. "Are you too crowded?"

"No, Dane, I'm not. I'm finding this new relationship quite spacious." I rolled over his legs and maneuvered my way back to my feet.

"Hennie?"

"Forget it. Just watch your show." I heard him sigh and shift off the couch to follow me. I went into the kitchen and opened the fridge. I stared at the sodas and reconsidered the choice. I was happy to be gaining my weight back, but I wasn't sure I wanted to overload my calories.

"Talk to me."

"I'm stuck in this house with you, and you are ignoring me."

"I'm not ignoring you!"

"Okay, you are ignoring my vagina."

"We discussed that."

"Yes, but we forgot to take bets on how long it would take for me to go insane in here."

"We don't have to stay home. We can go out."

"No, I can't risk you being noticed. Without my core magic to back up my spells, they're just wiccan wishes."

"Well then, what do you want me to do?"

"Not be so damn calm!" I slammed the fridge door and crossed my arms.

He smiled and crossed his arms as well. "I would be flattered, but I don't think this has anything to do with me."

"Oh, okay, because there is someone else here to be mad at."

"Well, that's the point, isn't it? The person you are really mad at isn't here, so I have to take the brunt of your anger."

"If Snake Eyes wants to show up, then I will be happy to dish out his fair share."

"I wasn't talking about him."

I turned back to the fridge and opened it again. Instead of grabbing for a soda, I grabbed one of Dane's beers. I popped open the top, but Dane ripped it out of my hands. "Are you kidding me?"

"Alcohol could be considered a crutch."

"Sex is a crutch. Alcohol is a crutch. What next, no refined sugar?" I pulled out a soda instead and popped it open. After a long draw, I looked back and found Dane was still watching me, his cool expression somewhere between anger and pity.

"When are you going to talk about this?" he asked.

"Talk about what?" I closed the fridge and took the long way around the island to get out of the kitchen. Naturally, Dane followed. I was finally getting more attention, but I didn't want it now.

"You've been avoiding it since the night we left."

"Avoiding what?" I tried to go upstairs, but Dane grabbed my arm.

"Not what, who. Rachel." He said the name almost in a whisper.

I took a breath. "She has nothing to do with this."

"She has everything to do with this. We should talk about this."

"There is nothing to discuss." I ripped my arm from him and proceeded upstairs.

Dane's feet clunked up the stairs. "She kicked you out of your coven. A coven that, by design, you are intimately linked to. Those women are in your blood, deeper than family."

"Thank you, Dane! I didn't need to be reminded of that."

"Why haven't you called her?"

"Oh, I don't know, perhaps the aforementioned exile."

"That coven needs you."

"No, it doesn't, because Rachel took over the big chair. She now has a direct beeline to the Big Guy."

"Since when?"

"Since that night." I attempted to push my bedroom door shut, but Dane just barreled his way through. As far as he was concerned, the bedroom was now mutual property.

"How do you know that?"

"Look, just drop it. Rachel has oodles of power now. Power she doesn't have to get from me and my trio of baggage. She doesn't need me. And she doesn't want me."

"And you're okay with that?"

"Of *course* I'm not okay with that. I wasn't okay with my best friend dying, but I couldn't do shit to stop that. I'm certainly not okay with being ditched by the only other friends in my life. What do you want, Dane? You want me to express my feelings? To tell you, I still feel them every time they do a spell and it rips my heart in two to not be included? Or maybe we should just focus on Rachel and

Paula. Let's talk about how they became my mentors after Sister Aggie died. Then Paula turned out to be the fucking devil in disguise. Now Rachel has become the opposing side of this power struggle and I'm stuck in between, not quite the good guy and not quite the bad guy, and yet somehow failing at both."

Dane snapped his fingers and pointed at me. "There! That's what's really bugging you."

"No, I'm pretty sure *you* are the one bugging me."

"You think you failed them, don't you?"

"Yes, I failed them. I was supposed to be doing the work of God, and I brought the devil to their doorstep."

Dane shook his head. "And what about me? Was I one of your failures?" I rolled my eyes. "If you had it all to do again, would you have set me free?"

"You're not free, Dane."

"Yes, Hennie, I am." He moved closer and pressed his hand to the side of my face. "Whether you believe it or not, you saved me from a living hell." I shifted away and busied myself straightening my bedspread. He moved up close behind me and pressed his hands down on my shoulders. "Because of you, I feel human."

I chuckled. "Ironic. It took the devil to make you feel human."

Dane tugged my shoulder, turning me to look at him. "It wasn't the devil that freed me. It was you and your coven. It was God's power." He unbuttoned my shirt.

"It wasn't God's power, it was Satan's power."

"And what is Satan?" Dane removed my shirt and undid my bra. I glanced down at his progress, unsure if he was seducing me or just being extremely helpful. "Come on,

Catholic school girl, what was the devil before he took up residence in hell?"

"An angel."

"And what sort of power does an angel possess?" Dane unbuttoned my pants and pushed them down around my knees, along with my panties. He pushed me down to sit on the bed and tugged them off entirely. "Is it good or evil?"

"It depends."

"Ah-ha." Dane raised his finger before removing his shirt and pants. "That's the point, then, isn't it? Power is neither good nor evil, but potentially both. You brought power to the coven when they had none."

"Finding my power exposed me to the devil." I scooted up on the bed and watched his fine form crawl up after me.

"Finding your power also brought me into your life." Dane settled in on top of me and kissed my chest.

"Yeah, and look how that turned out."

Dane lifted his head and frowned at me. I bit back my smile. "Was that a joke?"

"Oh, you finally recognized one of those, did you?"

Dane smiled a genuine smile. "You know you are in a very compromising position to be taunting me?"

"Oh, yeah?" I teased. "What, pray tell, will you do to me?"

Dane smiled and pushed my hands up over my head. He pinned my wrists in one hand and dragged the other one down my body. He paused, looking at my face for signs of discomfort when he reached my hip, but I wasn't afraid of him. Unfortunately, I should have been.

Dane bypassed the remainder of my body and grabbed my foot. I squealed as he tortured the sensitive skin. He chuckled as I squirmed and writhed. I pulled one hand free, but it didn't offer any more leverage against his muscular weight.

Somewhere in the process of trying to get my foot away from him, he entered me. My concerns about my feet melted away, and I relaxed back against the bed. I closed my eyes and wrapped my legs around him, pulling his tensing hips deeper into me.

I opened my eyes again and found a new lover on top of me. Paul was affixed to my body, pushing against me, sending ripples of dark energy through me along with my impending climax. I cried out for Dane and closed my eyes again.

"You okay?" he asked, leaning in closer.

I nodded and opened my eyes. I was once again with Dane. "I love you."

He paused momentarily in his movement, but continued slightly more rhythmically. I kept my eyes on him, watching him watching me. For the first time since our sexual encounters had begun, I felt like I was with Dane. Not with a reformed bad boy. Not with a demon hunter. Just Dane.

And it was magical.

CHAPTER 14

"Y OU'RE SMILING AGAIN." DANE smirked at me from across the table. We had decided to have our coffee in the dining room that morning. As usual, Dane engrossed himself in his newspaper, and I focused on my crossword puzzle. It was so pathetically normal that it kept making me smirk.

"Sorry." I chuckled and straightened my mouth.

"Don't apologize, I don't think I've seen you smile this much since... possibly never."

"You should have met me before I found out I was the embodiment of Satan. I was really fun then."

Dane smiled at me. "Did you really mean what you said last night? Or were you just in the heat of the moment?"

I looked down at my pen and scribbled a heart on the newspaper. "I think so."

"Maybe you should try it on in the daylight. See if it fits."

I licked my lips and looked across the table at him. I could see the anticipation in his eyes. He wanted me to feel for him as he felt for me. More and more I did. I couldn't pinpoint when it had changed. Perhaps getting the bulk of the hell out of my veins had opened my eyes to the subtle tenderness in his manner. Opened me up to the way a balanced relationship should be. Equal, honest, and forgiving. I opened my mouth to speak the words. "I—"

The back door crashed open, making me jump. Dane was on his feet in a second, ready to fight the demon invasion, but the dark shadows pouring into the kitchen weren't from hell.

"FBI! Get down!" the men in black yelled as they surrounded the table. More filed in from the living room and I could hear others on the stairs invading every room of my home. They aimed handguns and rifles at both of us as we slowly kneeled down on the floor.

Before I could get my body down low enough for them, they grabbed my arm and cuffed my wrist. They yanked my other arm, twisting it uncomfortably and forcing a yelp from me.

"Leave her alone!" Dane bucked back up, but one of the men put his knee into his back, forcing him down again. "She doesn't know anything!" Dane stared across the linoleum. "She doesn't know anything about me," he repeated quieter, as if advising me not to admit anything.

The men lifted me to my feet and ushered me away. They took me outside to a black sedan and shoved me in the back seat. I watched them take Dane away in a similar fashion, but in addition to the handcuffs, they had gagged him and restrained his feet. They weren't taking any chances that he would get away a second time.

"Tsk, tsk, tsk," my shadow's tongue clicked. I looked up to the rearview mirror, where I could see his serpentine form sitting next to me. "Oh Hennie, I'm not sure you are going to get out of this pickle without using your magic. I hope when the time comes, I'm feeling more generous to you than you have been to me."

CHAPTER 15

I SAT IN A green plastic chair, staring across the police station. The FBI was in the captain's office reliving their epic criminal catch. It would only be a matter of time before they removed Dane from the interrogation room and took him back to prison. I wondered how long it would take to get his death sentence back on schedule.

"So, you didn't know this guy was Dane Pratchett?" the officer asked from behind his desk. His questions had been getting progressively more sarcastic and snider.

"I knew his name, but I didn't know he was a criminal."

"So, you were shacking up with this guy for months and didn't have any clue he was a wanted fugitive?"

"That's correct."

"Oh, this is lame, Hennie," my shadow said to me through the reflection in the officer's framed picture of his wife and kids. "Just use your magic. Here, I'll give you a little help."

I felt a kick of juice push into my veins against my will. Much like a reformed junkie, the tiny dose felt like coming home again. I resisted the urge to grab onto it or use it.

"You don't own a television or a radio?"

"I do, but I don't watch the news."

"Or read a newspaper. Or converse with other human beings ever."

"I'm not very social."

"And yet you met this guy and let him into your home."

"What do you want me to say?" I shrugged. "He was a one-night stand that turned into more. I'm sorry I didn't keep up with the local news, but do you really think I would have let a man who murders women in my life if I knew he did such things?"

"You wouldn't think so," my shadow interjected.

The officer made a note in his report and pulled a photo from his file. "So, who exactly is this?"

I stared down at the photo of me in full sister mode: robe, habit, and veil—a surveillance photo of me and Meredith taken at the prison before Dane's mysterious disappearance. The image was grainy, but there wouldn't be a lot of wiggle room if they could establish I was a member of a convent at the time. Unless Meredith and I could corroborate that Dane was there when we left. However, since neither of us was on video leaving the prison, that put a damper on our defense.

"I don't know," I claimed.

"That's you, sweetheart." The officer poked my face in the photo.

I looked again and shook my head. "I admit there is a likeness. I mean, in that I also have a nose and mouth."

"Don't play around with me, missy. This is you."

"No, it isn't," I insisted. "You can't even see the hairline or the neck. That could literally be any white girl in North America."

"This is you!" The officer poked the photo again.

I opened my mouth to retort my singular defense, but someone did it for me.

"No, it isn't."

I looked back to see who was helping my case, and I saw Ruby dressed in her fatigues—or at least the Catholic version of them. Her pale skin and hard-earned cleft lip were her most notable features, but I would never again make the mistake of calling her shy. She had a sharp edge beneath her sullen exterior, one that was also hard-earned.

"Tell Ruby I love her husband's work," my shadow said.

"Who the hell are you?" the officer asked Ruby.

"I am Sister Ruby. The photo you possess is of two of our members. Sister Meredith and Sister Erin."

"Oh yeah? And can you produce these women to prove it?"

"I can produce one of them. Sadly, Sister Erin died several months ago." Ruby pulled out a paper clipping and handed it to the officer. He examined it and shook his head.

"She died before this photo was taken."

"Are you sure?"

"Yeah, this says..." The officer looked at the date on the surveillance photo. He looked back at the newspaper clipping, then back at the photo. "This was taken the same day," he said, frowning. "I thought... How did your sister die?"

"It looked like suicide. At least that's what the coroner determined at the time. The truth is, we were baffled by the incident. When we heard about your escaped inmate, we thought it might have to do with her visit to the prison that day."

"Wait a minute." The officer slapped down the photo. "You mean you are just coming forward with this now? Today?"

"I'm afraid we've had a streak of bad luck at the convent: deaths and a fire. I'd be happy to answer any questions—"

"We've been looking for this guy for almost a year and you conveniently show up today."

"The Lord works in mysterious ways." Ruby smiled.

"Can I go now?" I asked, clanking my handcuffs.

"No!" the officer yelled at me. "We are still charging you for aiding and abetting."

"You won't do that," Ruby said.

"Why the hell not?" the officer asked.

"Because she is the victim."

"Victim!"

"Don't you remember how Dane viciously attacked her?"

The officer looked back at me and frowned.

"He would have killed her if you hadn't shown up."

The officer's eyes glazed over and he reached out to touch my hand. "He will never hurt you again," he said in an almost monotone voice.

"You saw how much pain he was causing her and you couldn't take it," Ruby continued.

"Murdering asshole," the officer mumbled.

"That's when you pulled the trigger."

"I shot him." The officer's mouth tugged up slightly into a smile that gave me chills.

"He's dead. His body is in the morgue."

"You bitch!" my shadow screamed. Ruby's eyes twitched in his direction as if she had heard him. She narrowed her eyes on the picture and the glass in the frame cracked into a spider web pattern that blocked his image from me. I stared at her in absolute awe of her talent.

"You are all going to go out and have drinks tonight," Ruby continued. "Celebrate the death of a murderer. Your report will reflect what happened. No one will look for him anymore. The news media will stop reporting on him. No one cares about a dead murderer."

"Yeah, motherfucking trash, that's what he was," the officer said, a more natural tone returning to his voice.

"Yeah, he was!" a passing officer added to his cheer with a high five and a whoop of his own. Before I knew it, the precinct was alive with the chatter of reliving the successful elimination of Dane, aka, "Pratchett the Hatchet."

I smiled at Ruby, amused by the surreptitious magic coursing through her. She was getting stronger. They were all getting so strong, not just as a group, but individually. I could feel it. I was proud, but also envious. They were moving on without me. They were fighting evil and saving souls.

Ruby gave my handcuffs a slight tug and released them to clank on the chair. I stood and encompassed her in a hug that she mostly returned. When I stepped back to greet her properly, I found her gaze fixed on something behind me. I turned back and saw Dane coming out of the interrogation room. He remained handcuffed, but no one was monitoring him. He spotted Ruby and slowed his approach. He stopped in front of her, shoulders squared as he lorded his height over her. "Hello, Ruby."

"Hello, Pratchett." Ruby's mouth thinned as she pinched her lips.

"Thanks for dropping by," he said.

"I didn't come for you. I came for the coven. We can't have ourselves being implicated with a murderer."

"No, of course not, especially when you were the ones who helped him escape." Dane smirked at her.

"Your release was a mistake," Ruby whispered.

Dane stepped a little closer, but Ruby didn't back down. "Then why save me a second time?"

"I told you—"

"Did Rachel send you?" I asked.

Ruby looked at me and then around at the officers. "We should get out of here. I don't want to disrupt the spell with contrary imagery."

We walked out of the precinct together. Ruby waved her hand at several cameras as we passed. The devices each gave off a popping sound, which resulted in their lights going off. I glanced at Dane to see what he thought of this, but he seemed content with the magic being tossed every which way.

We emerged from the police station as the cloud cover finally released its rain. We ran through the pummeling shower to reach Ruby's car. When she opened her driver's side door, she paused and looked back at me. "I'm glad you're doing better, Hennie."

Ruby ducked down into her car and slammed the door. I reached for the door handle on the passenger side, but she hadn't unlocked it. The car's engine started and Ruby drove away. "What the hell?" I threw my arms out at the distancing car. "It's a monsoon out here!"

"Come on, Hennie. We can hoof it." Dane tugged on my arm.

"No!" I stomped my foot. "I refuse to be treated like a goddamn leper! I didn't even want to be a part of their stupid coven. Aggie brought me in! She wanted me there. She thought I could be better!" I poked my finger at myself. "And I tried!" My eyes welled with tears, mixing in with the rain pouring down my face. Dane moved to embrace me, but I pulled away. "We exorcised the demons. We healed the sick. We made you into a good man," I squawked. "I saved them all! I did everything they ever asked of me!"

"I know," Dane whispered.

"Then why do they hate me so much?" I broke down and Dane swooped in again, pulling me to his chest.

"They don't hate you, Hennie. They're just afraid of you."

"I'm afraid of me, too."

"I know." Dane kissed the top of my head and squeezed me a little tighter.

CHAPTER 16

"WHERE ARE WE?" I asked Paula when we entered the bowling alley. For this rare occasion, she wore normal clothing. It was a pleasant change, but it made me nervous. It meant there was a reason she didn't want people to see her as a nun.

Who didn't like nuns? Bad guys? Guilty people? Satanists?

"Just relax, Hennie. I know you've had a tough week." She walked us through the main area across the alleys where a few families were getting in a game before the leagues started. "Well, tough life in general. I can see why you've turned away from the magic I'm offering you."

"Because it's as addictive as crack cocaine."

"The addiction is controllable, assuming you restrain yourself. Let's face it, you do tend to dive into the deep end even for the little things."

"So now it's my fault."

"Don't get me wrong, I could have restrained it a little more, but you really are fun to watch when you go black-eyed bitch." Paula turned, taking us alongside the lanes.

"If you are going to try to trick me into using my magic again, it won't work."

"I know you're happy with your little life. However, short of getting a day job, you are going to have to start using some magic to get ahead in life."

"Are you offering me a job?"

"I'm offering you the same job you have always had. The only one you agreed to do for me." Paula opened the door leading behind the pin equipment. "You are going to be my conscience." I reluctantly entered the dark room.

We maneuvered past the clanking of the pinsetters to an open area. There was a table set for three—two on one side and one on the other. It wasn't much more than a folding table, but the stack of papers and old-fashioned inkwell looked fancy.

"You are going to have an opportunity to use your power for good, as you would prefer to." Paula took a seat at the table and offered me a chair next to her. "Come sit."

"What is this?"

"We are taking clients today. Each client will ask for our help. You will decide whether they deserve it."

"Help?" I laughed. "You want to *help* people?"

"For a fee."

"Their soul?"

"Oh, please, I can barely stand my own soul. What good would it do me to have more of them?"

"What's the price?" I asked.

"Anything I want. It's a debt to be filled as needed."

"Like mass murder?"

"It's not an irrational debt. It is equivalent to the favor they receive."

"But they won't know what the debt is."

"Life is a balancing act. I can't disrupt too many threads or Daddy gets angry. The opportunity to repay a debt might come years later. And as good as I am at foretelling, I can't see as far as I would like or to the specifications I would like. Damn free will and all."

"What if—?"

"Hennie, you can say no, just sit!"

I sat down in the folding chair and glared at Paula. "Now what?"

"Hello?" a man said from the seat across from us, making me jump. He had come out of nowhere.

"How did you...?" I trailed off, glancing at Paula. There was no point questioning the how. I straightened my chair to face the man. He was perhaps in his fifties, though life had made him more frail than strong.

"What can I do for you?" Paula asked the man.

At first, he waffled, not being able to decide if he wanted anything. But then he broke into tears. The man sobbed for a minute, unable to speak. When he finally calmed himself, Paula handed him a tissue and stroked his hand gently. I hated that she was as good at playing the good guy as the bad. I also hated that some part of me missed the woman she'd pretended to be for me.

"It's my wife," the man sputtered out. "She has cancer. A brain tumor. Inoperable. The doctors have given her three months to live. I want her to recover. I want her to be cured. No more cancer. No more disease ever."

"I can do what you ask, but there will be a price. A debt to be paid at a later date."

"I don't care."

"Wait," I interrupted. "Do you know who you are asking this favor from?"

The man looked at me, and then at Paula. "Yes, I do."

"And you are willing to be indebted to her?"

"Of course. I love my wife."

"Have you tried praying?" I asked, though I knew what his answer would be.

"I have prayed nonstop for months. I don't wish to be blasphemous, but God has never given me a sit-down meeting."

"He's not wrong." Paula grimaced. "He doesn't even return my phone calls and I'm his firstborn."

I stared at her, shaking my head. "I don't even know if you're joking. Is this how you normally conduct business? On a card table in the back of a bowling alley?"

"I usually do it in a pizzeria, but I couldn't stop myself from ordering pizza. Acid reflux, eck." She thumped her chest.

"Seriously? This is not funny. A man's wife is hanging in the balance and you are making a mockery of it."

"I am not making a mockery of it, Hennie. This..." Paula waved her hands to encompass everything. "...is for your benefit. This man is not going to remember this. In his mind, he is praying to me. I'm just having us act it out so you can interpret it in your little human brain. Now, what is your decision?"

"About what?"

"Does his wife live or die?"

"You can heal her with a snap of your fingers," I said.

"Is that your decision?"

"What's the debt?"

"I... don't... know."

"I can't decide without knowing what you are going to do to him."

"He's fine with it. It doesn't matter what you think."

"Sir, listen to me. She is evil. She could, in turn, give *you* cancer."

Paula scoffed. "Why would I do that?"

"I don't care," the man assured me. "As long as my wife lives a long and happy life."

"Okay, that's sweet, but what if she turns out to be sleeping with your best friend and, years from now, you hate her guts and wish she were dead, anyway?"

The man frowned at me and glanced at Paula. "Is she saying no?"

"Not yet," Paula said. "Explain to her what the rationale behind your decision is."

The man sniffled and his eyes watered. He looked at me, a few of his tears dropping on the table. "My wife is an exceptional singer, and she can dance too. She plays the piano, and she works with the kids down at the rehab clinic. She helps a lot of people. I know why God has called her home. She is a beautiful soul, but I think she has more to do here on Earth. I don't care if I die, or if she leaves me. She is an exceptional woman, and I think she deserves a chance to do as much good on this Earth as she can."

I could feel the man's pain. It wasn't just empathy; I could feel it as if it were my own. The only thing more overwhelming than his sorrow was his love for his wife. I blinked away my own tears and looked at Paula. "What is this?" I motioned to my uncontrolled response to the man's emotions.

She shrugged. "The burden of a soul. What is your response? Does she live or die?"

As I looked down at my hands. I could feel my power prickling beneath my skin. The part of me that was addicted to it was rationalizing its use. I wouldn't be hurting anyone. I would be saving a life. That wasn't evil. That was noble and heroic.

Halfway into my imaginary cape and tights, I remembered what the man had said. God was calling his wife home. The man's reason for saving his wife was so she could do more here on Earth. It sounded to me like she had done plenty already. It was time someone took over for her.

I looked up at the man across from me and allowed my resolve to harden my features. "What you are asking for is the same thing every man asks for when their time of passing is near. Your wife may well be a good person, but if God wants her, then I will not stand in his way." I turned my mirthless gaze to Paula. "Nor will I allow my power to be used as a fountain of youth for every sick human." I turned back to the old man, who was weeping harder, his agony as fresh in my heart as it was in his. I bolstered the last of my strength to keep my declaration as stony as my face. "The answer is no."

The man faded into oblivion and with him went the ache in my heart.

"That was cold," Paula said, her voice hoarse with drama. "And consider the source." She motioned to herself. "I can't believe you let someone die to avoid using your magic."

"Don't!" I threw a finger in her face. "You might think this game is clever, but I don't. You put hope in him and then forced me to rip it away. I might be the one knocking down the pins..." I motioned back to the bowling mechanism conveniently behind me. "...but you are the one who keeps setting them back up."

"It's only cruel if you say no."

"It is not my place to decide who lives or dies!"

"This coming from the girl who saved that terminal boy in the hospital."

"That was different. I was using—"

"You thought you were using God's power, so it was okay, right? You heard that man, Hennie. My power may not be without strings, but at least it's available. God's a busy guy. If you really want to do something good with your power, then you need to start considering that sometimes heroes have to get blood on their hands." Paula pushed out her chair and stood. "See you tomorrow. Maybe you'll be in a more sympathetic mood." She winked and left me to contemplate fine lines and the quagmires that inevitably push people over them.

CHAPTER 17

THE HOSPITAL WASN'T SO much a medical facility as a renovated sanitarium. From the outside, it looked like an idealistic old building—a two-story red brick structure with tall pane-glass windows. There were even decorative arches over them, easing the otherwise hard lines of the architecture. Despite that, though, my eyes drifted to the basement windows. There was always something creepy going on in the basements of these places.

On the inside, the building's age was a little more obvious. It had a smell that could only be described as clinical and old. Pale green paint covered the walls in the foyer and hallways. Behind the visitors' station, set against the back wall of the lobby, was a set of concrete stairs covered in rubber tread mats. At no specific points from the beginning or the ending of the stairwell, the paint turned to a peach color. I wasn't sure if there was any reason for this other than reminding people which floor they were on. I had no doubt that a building of this size with repetitive rooms could become a confusing maze if you didn't pay attention.

Though in slight disrepair, the hospital looked bright and clean. The receptionist behind the oversized counter at the visitors' station gave Dane and me a warm smile and waved us over. I glanced at Dane before heading over to her. He followed slightly behind me, making it a point to keep his head down and not look the woman directly in the eyes, in case the young woman might recognize him from the newspapers or the endless online campaigns to bring him to justice.

"You must be here for Paula?" the petite redhead asked.

I looked her over, suspicious of what her part in this little game was going to be. She wasn't wearing a habit and robe, so I knew she wasn't officially a nun, but I was certain she was probably an aspirant. Something about giving every second of her life to good deeds and God appealed to this young woman. I wanted to tell her it was all a lie. I wanted to tell her that the devil permeated every aspect of human culture. But who was I to talk, standing two feet away from a serial killer and embodying the essence of the devil in a hijacked body?

"Paula told you about us?" I asked.

The woman smiled even brighter, if that was possible. There is a gap between her front teeth she didn't seem the least bit self-conscious about. "She described you pretty well, and I took a guess."

I twisted my jaw, thinking of how Paula might have described us to the young girl. It was probably easy enough to pick out the blond girl with black-tipped hair, a nose ring, and her six-foot log of a boyfriend. "Do you know where we can find her?"

"Of course." The girl beamed now, practically glowing with Christian countenance. "Sister Paula always visits the terminally ill when she comes. She provides them with much-needed counseling during their painful ascent."

"Do you have a lot of terminally ill people here?" Dane asked over my shoulder.

The girl looked back at him, and her smile dimmed. Not in a suspicious way or a frightened way, but more like she simply lost her train of thought. She blinked and her mouth opened, but it was several seconds before she stuttered out any words. "We do provide hospice to a good number of people on a regular basis. When life is at its most futile, it's important that our faith is strengthened so we are prepared for our journey toward God." The girl's smile returned, but it was more cockeyed this time, like she had forgotten how the muscles in her face worked. "I can take you to Paula if you like?" Though I was certain the invitation was meant for both of us, she never took her eyes off Dane.

"That's quite all right." I shifted my feet, forcing myself back into the woman's line of sight. "Why don't you just point us in the most likely direction?"

The woman blinked as if coming out of hypnosis and put back on her warm and friendly, albeit technically fake, smile. "Of course." She looked back at the clock on the wall behind her. "She should be upstairs by now. Just head up the stairs and go south into the yellow section. I'm sure you'll catch up with her there."

I gave her a curt nod and thanked her before heading up the stairs. The cold metal railing was part rust, part paint, but the years of unintentional hand-polishing had left it smooth. I turned back to check on Dane and noticed he hadn't yet left the lobby. The young woman had caught his arm and was saying something more to him. He listened carefully, and then his brow furrowed deeply. I turned back to see what this intrigue might be about, but then

Dane smiled and shook his head. He offered the girl an apology and walked away. With a half-cocked smile still on his face, he reached the stairs. He caught sight of me and his smile disappeared.

"What was that all about?"

"That was interesting." He jogged up the steps past me and kept right on going.

I followed behind him, even more perturbed than when I had caught the woman giving him googly eyes. "What do you mean, interesting?" I asked, trying to sound disinterested.

"I mean, she's an interesting girl." We reached the second floor and the peach walls spread off to our left, while a new pale yellow color painted the walls to our right.

"What did she say to you?"

Dane smirked at me and started heading down the yellow hallway. "I don't think I should tell you, given your current state of rehabilitation."

We passed by several rooms, each a mirror image of the last. I had been right that it would be easy to get lost in this place. Each room contained a single bed beneath a hanging crucifix. Most of the rooms housed frail and disheveled patients, either sleeping or staring vacantly across the room. Each one was dealing with their own version of a medical hell. Loud beeping heart monitors, rasping ventilators, humming blood pressure monitors permeated the hallway along with intermittent bursts of coughing and hacking. I didn't want to think about how many of the people on this floor might never leave it again. Death was a part of life, but as someone who was never meant to be alive, I found the topic particularly frightening. After all, there was no heaven for me. My ticket was straight back to hell, no matter how good I was topside.

"Wait." I stopped walking and turned to Dane. "What exactly did she say?"

"As much as I enjoy your jealousy, now is not the time."

"This is not jealousy," I lied. "This is curiosity. I was just wondering what she had said to put such a big smile on your face. It must've been something pretty special since you barely crack a smile at my jokes."

"Oh, I don't think she was joking." The same cockeyed smile came back to his face, and I felt a tingle in my fingertips.

"She didn't?" I could hear the depth in my voice, a low threatening rumble that didn't quite sound like me. "She propositioned you, didn't she?"

Dane chuckled. "I turned her down."

My control tore apart at the seams. I felt the energy inside of me being fueled by my anger. It didn't matter that Dane had refused her. All that mattered was she had asked. The audacity. The degrading violation of my emotions and my territory were blinding my judgment.

I turned back, hungry for revenge. Prepared for a fight, though I knew there would be no fight. It would be a massacre—me shredding apart some poor innocent woman because she had the gall to appreciate a fine man.

I practically made it back to the stairwell before Dane's arm wrapped around my waist and lifted me off my path. We spun, his feet dancing and my legs kicking out from beneath me. He threw me out of his arms and I nearly collided with an elderly gentleman lying in his hospital bed. Fortunately, he was under heavy sedation along with all of his machines and gizmos that were keeping him alive—very little emphasis on *alive*.

When I got my bearings and turned back to face Dane, he had closed the door to the room, leaving us alone, with respect to the comatose patient. I tried to barrel past him, not even considering the differences between our strengths. He wrapped me up in his arms, pinning mine down against my side and crushing me against his chest.

"Let me go! I need to teach that bitch a lesson."

Dane shushed me gently and rocked me back and forth as if we were slow dancing. I bucked against his arms, but there was no hope of getting away unless I planned on using my power against him.

"Jealousy is a very powerful motivator," he said in a soothing voice. "It's a direct correlation to love, so even when there is no logic behind it, it's rational to the heart."

"This isn't about jealousy."

"This is about love. This is about feelings you aren't quite ready to admit because they don't fit into that normal little life you always wanted to have. But more importantly, this is about Paula capitalizing on that emotion so she can lure you into an uncontrolled use of your magic."

"Paula?" I relaxed in his arms as I felt the anger leave my system. "She planted the attraction in her mind. Like a literal booby-trap."

"Well, I'd like to believe that *some* of the attraction was natural," Dane added, slightly sullen.

"I have no doubt it was. You obviously were able to resist the bait. Too bad *I* wasn't."

"You have nothing to be ashamed of. Clearly, this is not going to be the first time we're faced with a challenge to our relationship. I'm sure everywhere we go I will be solicited for my services."

"Shut up." I scoffed and sloughed his arms off me. I slipped around him, back to the door. Before I could get it open, he grabbed my hand and tugged me back. I thought he might try to sneak in a tryst to prove his affections for me, but the look on his face was stern.

"I have no interest in other women. I want you to know that, in case it would be something that would worry you from time to time."

I wanted to be flattered. I wanted to be filled with the warmth of love. I cared for Dane, and I probably loved him, regardless of whether I admitted it, but our relationship stemmed from something chaotic and unnatural—two evils reborn as something good. It was true there was probably no one else on Earth that could understand the trials I had to go through to maintain the smallest vestige of my humanity. It was also true that without him, I would have been lost already. He had become a life preserver in the midst of this addiction, and I was so grateful for his support and his devotion.

And yet there was still a tiny little piece of me that wondered if two people, created from the blood and misery of others, even deserved to have love.

CHAPTER 18

A S WE CONTINUED DOWN the hall in search of Paula, the sounds of beeps and bleeps subsided. We were coming into a section that no longer required extraneous methods to keep the patients alive. This was the hospice and terminally ill section. I knew from the building's design that there was nothing different about this end of the wing. However, it felt like the walls swallowed the sunlight before it could make it through the windows. The warmth of the old boiler system didn't seem to penetrate the rooms here.

As we passed a set of windows looking into old operatories, I could see the reflection of the adjacent rooms in the glass. I stopped when I noticed a dark shadow swirling around the patient inside. The elderly woman looked to be in anguish. She pinched her eyes shut and twisted her fists into her sheets. The dark entity dipped down his amorphous head to the woman. I could hear him speak to her, nothing more than a susurration, but I sensed it was an offering. It was a low blow to solicit someone so desperate, but I could expect nothing less of a demon.

I looked over at Dane to see if he was going to do anything about the uninvited guest, but the look on his face was not angst or anger, it was disappointment. Before

I could ask what he was thinking, he rested his hand on the small of my back and pushed me forward. "This has nothing to do with us."

Since Dane was predisposed to hunt demons, I could only assume this was one of those situations where a predator can be a blessing.

I noticed another dark shadow swirling around a patient in one of the rooms a little ways down. The man within turned to look at me. He reached out a bony, wavering hand and croaked out a plea for help. For a moment, I wondered if I was capable of helping him. It wasn't the type of help I wanted to give. It wasn't the type of help *anyone* wanted to give. And yet we freely gave to lesser species to ease their discomfort. It was an argument that had been won and lost over and over again: free will versus the Hippocratic oath.

This shadow didn't seem to solicit the man so much as watch him. I wasn't sure demons sought entertainment in the mortal world, but once again, I supposed I couldn't apply any morality to a demon. The shadow noticed me as I had him. It tipped its head, as if trying to fathom what I was, the possessed or the possessor. It didn't matter what I was; I was just wrong to him. An abnormality even among the abnormal.

We walked on and finally caught sight of a black robe and veil leaning over an especially pale patient. Paula was praying for the man as his mouth widened and closed like a fish gasping for breath on land. I listened in on the words she was saying and I realized she was giving the man his last rites. I half expected the words to be tainted with some backhanded terminology or a hidden Satanic phrasing, but I had heard it more than once during my stint with my coven and she was saying it correctly.

Several minutes later, the man's mouth stopped moving and Paula finished her recitation. She made the sign of the cross, placed the man's hands over his chest, and slid her hand down his face, closing his eyelids. When she turned back around and saw us standing in the doorway, she gave us a somber smile. "They all slip away eventually, don't they?" The tone of her voice should have been sarcastic, but she was saying it's almost wistfully.

"What the hell do you think you're doing?" I asked, thoroughly disgusted by the display.

"What do you mean?"

"Do you seriously come here regularly and put on this ridiculous performance?"

Paula sighed and rubbed her forehead. "I know it's difficult for you to comprehend this, but there are times when it is appropriate to offer mercy to one's enemy."

"And this is you offering mercy to your enemies? Last rites to a dying man?"

"This is the only time I offer mercy." Paula motioned back to the now dead man lying on the bed behind her. "There's no point in fighting for the soul of a dead man. There's no use in possessing an empty body. And there's no pleasure in frightening a man who is already terrified of his fate."

I narrowed my eyes and waited for the sarcastic, snide or passive aggressive comments that should've come after her almost considerate statement. But it never came. Paula stared at me, waiting for me to digest the load of crap she was throwing at me. Rather than frazzle my already tenuous hold on my anger, I shook away my resentment for her two-faced behavior. There were too many faces to count already.

"Why did you ask me to come here? And please don't tell me you want me to be a candy-striper."

"I have a project I need your assistance with."

"A project? I'm not going to get duped into using my magic."

"You don't have to use your magic if you don't want to. Though I don't imagine it would be possible not to at least try."

"How's that again?" I asked.

Paula looked around and found a dispenser on the wall. She took a heavy squirt of hand sanitizer from it and started rubbing it between her fingers and over her palms. "Come with me." She pushed between us and walked further down the yellow hallway. I rolled my eyes at Dane and followed behind her.

"Where are we going?" I asked when I noticed there were no longer patients in the rooms we passed. Eventually we reached a section where both walls had transitioned to long lines of head-level windows, giving us views into the large rooms within. It didn't take much of a history lesson to know that these were the TB wards, areas of the hospital where they would cluster the tuberculosis patients to help contain the communicable disease.

Though I was certain the room was once bright and sterile like the rest of the hospital, these sections were severely disused. The lack of maintenance left paint chipping off the walls, tiles bowing, and instead of replacing the broken windows, they had covered them with wood.

"I need your help with something, Hennie," Paula finally said.

"Since when do you need my help? If this is one of your tricks—"

Paula stopped in her tracks and whipped around to face me. "I only wish this was a trick. I wish I didn't have to ask for your help. The fact that I have to is more degrading than you can ever imagine, but it is important, so I am willing to put aside my ego for the sake of the greater good."

I snorted and sputtered out a laugh.

"Since when do you care about the greater good?" Dane asked, since I was laughing too hard to do it myself.

Paula shifted away from us, rubbing her hands together. At first, I thought she was just rubbing away more of the hand sanitizer, but as I watched her longer, I realized she was wringing her hands, twisting them in a nervous or uncomfortable way. I had never seen Paula exhibit symptoms of uneasiness, not even when she was playing the part of my mentor and friend. She had always been a pinnacle of calm strength.

"Something's happened," she said.

"What is it?" I asked for what seemed like the twelfth time, but this time I was legitimately interested in the answer.

"I'm not quite sure what it is yet. But it could be bad."

"Bad for whom?"

"Bad for everyone. Bad for the entire world. Bad for..." Paula trailed off and looked down the hallway. Since the building's construction, there had been a series of successive renovations adding extensions to the wings. Ahead of us was a slight bend where the new addition slanted west to accommodate for the property line. "You can't just pull a string and not expect to unravel the whole ball of yarn."

I wasn't sure if Paula was talking to me or herself, but either way it was coming out as riddles, and I didn't understand one bit of it. She seemed to be losing focus. Her mind was elsewhere. I moved over to her and rested my hand on her arm. She looked over at me, and for a moment, she looked like Paula. The woman I used to know. The woman I'd thought she was.

"Your reality, human reality, is designed around specific laws of motion—physics. To you, they are simply facts of life. To me, however, they are fences—a designated set of boundaries to keep you safe and predictable. I can jump the fence anytime I want. I am not bound by time or space. I'm free to move fluidly through the universe untethered by the mortal realm if I wish."

As interesting as this all was, it still sounded like satanic propaganda. I knew Paula was able to pop in and out as she pleased. I had seen my shadow stop time. This wasn't new to me. "Paula, you need to focus. What's changed? Why is your fluidity suddenly so important?"

All at once, Paula seemed to snap back into reality, or at least back into my reality. She looked at Dane and with a stern voice said, "You'll need to stay with her. Don't leave her side, no matter what you see or feel."

I threw my arms up in a shrug. "For the love of God, what is going on?" I was so sick of asking the question.

"Follow the hallway down to the end. There are a series of laboratories in the last section. The patient was brought in several weeks ago. The symptoms being reported were initially manic behavior and hallucinations resulting in violent encounters with friends and family. The behavior has since changed. She is now calm, but the incidents occurring around her have forced the staff to move her to the farthest section of the building in order to protect the other patients."

"You want me to go down that hallway and check on a patient? And then what? Do an exorcism? Or should I go straight to the lobotomy?"

"You're welcome to try either or both, but I don't think you will get very far. I just need you to observe and report back to me." Paula turned and started heading back up the hall where we had come from.

"You're not even going to come with me? Who's gonna be my cheerleader?" Despite the taunts, Paula did not turn back to glare at me. She kept walking down the hallway, separating herself as quickly as possible from the situation. I looked at Dane for an answer. "Is it just me or is she being super weird today?"

Dane was staring down the hallway before us. Although there was nothing to see past the bend, his gaze was intense. "There's something down there," he said in a low, predatory tone. It made me think of hairs bristling up on the back of a wolf when he met with an opponent he knew he was going to have to fight.

CHAPTER 19

I HADN'T GIVEN THE situation its due credit. Frankly, I had been through so much the last few months—hell, the last few *years*—that I was tired of being surprised by how much shittier my life could get. I stalked down the hallway, refusing to be intimidated by the mere suggestion of a threat. I had been fighting demons, devils, and my own shadow for too long to be bothered by a victim of possession. However, the closer we got to our destination, the more I realized Dane was right. There was definitely something down here.

"Stay close to me," Dane warned when I got a few steps ahead of him.

I glanced back and saw that his eyes were still cold and attentive, like he was hunting someone or something. Without mirrors or a reflective surface, I couldn't see what he was seeing, but something had him on edge. The same way Paula had been on edge.

We reached the bend, which was separated by a set of swinging double doors. To be safe, I peeked through the foggy windows to ensure there weren't a series of pitfalls awaiting us on the other side. Dane did the same, but didn't report anything to be concerned about. Other than the obvious one.

"You don't feel it, do you?" Dane examined me carefully.

I blinked at him, trying to decide if now was a good time in our relationship to start lying.

"What do you feel?" I asked, changing the subject.

Dane took a breath and looked at the double doors. "I feel alive." I perked a brow at him. "Just on the cusp of death, but still alive."

"Cusp of death, huh?" I nodded. "This should be interesting." I put my hands on the swinging doors.

"What does it feel like to you?" he asked, not letting the subject drop.

I thought about it for a moment. I understood what he meant about feeling alive, but he meant it from the perspective of a near-death experience. Walking on the edge of a deep precipice, knowing that at any moment a strong breeze could snatch away your life. In his feral state of kill-or-be-killed, he found the feeling exhilarating, but it wasn't meant to be.

To the sane person, it was meant to be repellent—a semi-tangible warning to all who entered. *Beware of the monsters within.* However, to me, it was something familiar. Frightening, to be sure. Raw and inhuman, but in a somewhat similar way as Dane, alluring to my senses.

"It feels like home," I answered and shoved the doors open. I caught a glimpse of a reflection in their small windows as they angled away from me. Dozens of wispy shadows surrounded Dane and me. They were hovering at the entrance. Waiting? Guarding? Or perhaps just enticed by the power within. Dane hadn't mentioned them, so I assumed they were the least of our worries.

As I stepped into the hallway that would ultimately lead to our possession victim, a thick cloud of silence surrounded me, blocking out all extraneous sounds. The lights above were the same fluorescent bulbs, but the glow barely reached me. The air should have been warm, but the temperature had dropped significantly. I could see my breath and with each exhale, the fog I created wrapped around a face only inches from mine.

Dane grabbed my hand and yanked it. I lurched back and hit his solid body. I looked up at his stony anger, which was directed at the empty space in front of us. I glanced between him and the vacancy, knowing my serpentine shadow must have been present and accounted for. I wished I could see him the way Dane could—if for no other reason than to make our conversations easier.

"That's what you think," Dane said to him. The ferocity in his voice made it clear that he was denying whatever it was my counterpart was babbling about. My shadow loved the sound of his own voice.

After a brief pause, the conviction of Dane's wrath melted slightly. Fear seeped into his eyes. "That's a lie." He glanced down at me. "I'm here to protect her." Dane's jaw tensed tightly. "We'll see about that," he said, getting the last word in. He moved forward, tugging me along with him.

"What did he have to say?" I asked, since it seemed to be important, and as usual, involved me.

Dane said nothing for several steps. "He was warning me that what you are about to attempt is dangerous and that I may not be able to keep you safe."

I had no doubt what Dane was saying was a factual statement. However, with regard to my question, I could tell it was a lie. Whatever he had been speaking to my shadow about, he didn't want to share it with me.

CHAPTER 20

I PUSHED OPEN THE white painted wood door. The room was longer than wide, designed to house at least a dozen patients on small cot beds. I could easily picture the nurses moving around the space in their white dress uniforms with those odd-shaped hats on their heads—emptying bedpans and giving sponge baths.

That was then.

Now the plaster walls were being held together by layers and layers of paint. The same paint that glued the old windows shut. The floors were new, but only by about a decade. Overhead, the ceiling tiles were turning brown from the leaks in the roof.

This wasn't a room for patients. This was, at best, a room to store old, outdated equipment. And yet there, at the far end of it, was a young girl sitting in a bed, propped up by pillows. Her eyes were bright and attentive, as if she were expecting us.

I moved forward, my feet cracking the occasional warped tile. Dane followed behind me.

At some point, I realized the girl was no closer and no farther than when I had started. I turned back to see if Dane had noticed our steps were accomplishing nothing.

I saw him in the distance, on the far side of the room. He hadn't followed me as I thought he had.

I shifted to look back at the girl, but I was no longer as distant as I had first perceived. I was at the very end of her bed. I could clearly see her long blond hair, freckled cheeks, and bright blue eyes.

I opened my mouth to speak to her, but she came at me, eyes feral and mouth gaping as a wretched torrent of screeching screams clawed at my eardrums. She collided with me and I dropped to the floor, pressed down by an enormous weight.

I landed and wrestled to remove the child, but she was gone. The only arms tangled in mine were Dane's. He was trying to help me up. "What's wrong?" he asked, searching the room for demons.

I huffed out a breath and looked past him to the girl. She was still sitting across the room in her bed. She hadn't moved an inch, and neither had I.

"What happened?"

I stood up and dusted myself off. "This is going to be a bit more difficult than I anticipated."

CHAPTER 21

I HAD NEVER IMAGINED I would feel air pressing against me the way water did when you go too deep. The thickness touched me in unnatural ways, the way my shadow could touch me, without actually making contact. Whatever resided inside of the little girl before me was a powerful creature, one that did not abide by the natural laws of the universe. One that I wasn't entirely sure should exist.

Had I taken two steps, or one, or none? I could no longer trust my eyes. Or my ears.

The sink on the far side of the room was dripping. Every slow plop was louder than the last. It would soon be deafening.

All the while, the girl before me sat stock still, staring at me, and through me. I had tried to reach her several times, but something was repelling me, forcing me to give up the task.

My senses had become my enemies. I was certain nothing in the room had changed during my attempts, but that didn't stop me from backpedaling away from an inexpiable extreme heat, or diving away from a sudden ceiling collapse. It was all in my mind, but of course that is the one thing you can't fight, no matter how hard you try.

In addition to the *plop, plop, plop* that was breaking the sound barrier, I could smell something rotting. I experienced the pungent aroma like a punch in the gut. My gag reflex jumped into overdrive, as if my body suspected this aroma was something I would consider eating. I tried to plug my nose, but the smell wasn't in the air, so breathing was not the issue.

I fell to my knees, eyes watering, mouth salivating uncontrollably. I coughed and heaved a few more times before gritting my teeth together and letting out a guttural scream.

I looked at the little girl in the bed and reached for my power. I reached deep to get the full arsenal. I wanted to knock this little twerp straight into hell.

I felt the power wrap around me, cloaking me like a shield. The smell instantly disappeared, the sound in the room returned to normal, and I walked forward without interruption.

I marched to the foot of the little girl's bed. She tipped her head slightly, but was otherwise unimpressed with my sudden resistance to her brainwashing.

"Get out!"

The girl slowly shook her head.

"Get... out!" I reached forward, pushing my power at the demon. I felt it go into the girl and her body jolted. For a moment, I felt her—a tiny whisper, no more than a cry in the dark from under her sheets, but she was there.

"No," the demon said through the girl.

I felt its power push back, and it reverberated against me. I tried to hold on, but the collision of our powers was too painful.

I stumbled back from the foot of the bed, heart racing and lungs burning. It felt like acid in my throat, and then I tasted the blood. Dane screamed at it to stop, but it wouldn't. I couldn't move. Everything hurt. My insides hurt.

Blood drained from my mouth and pool on the floor. I wanted it to be in my head, but I knew even if it was, it was still real enough to kill me.

I couldn't run away. Whatever had hold of me was not letting go. I had thrown the entirety of hell at it, and it wasn't budging. Fire against fire wouldn't work.

I only had one option left. It was a long shot, and one that would ultimately result in a confrontation I wanted even less than my current one, but it was either fight or die.

I reached out for my sisters.

CHAPTER 22

I T WAS QUITE POSSIBLY the equivalent of magical rape. I used my hell-fueled power to strengthen my tether to the sisters of my former coven. I shoved it through, forcing them to connect with each other and then to me.

I could feel each of them, stunned and distraught as the unwelcome presence grabbed onto them, demanding their attention, and drawing them into an impromptu magical trance. Their power sifted into me, one by one, each a distinct, albeit small, puzzle piece in the coven. They were beautiful and so strong, and touching them in this way made me miss them all the more.

I reached the final piece of the puzzle and I bolstered my bravado. Rachel was more than a coven member; she was beholden to a great power. A power that, in theory, was the seed of all magical energy. If she couldn't get the monster off me, then no one could.

I felt Rachel's resistance, but I had not taken this path with permissions in mind. I pushed through, finalizing the connection and bringing the wrath of God down on the enemy before me.

There was a bright flash of light, and I felt claws ripping at me, but that was the end of it: the fight, the connection, and my consciousness.

CHAPTER 23

I FELT DANE'S HANDS and his lips kissing my hand. "Come on, Hennie," he whispered. "Please, God, don't let this be her end."

I opened my eyes and found him kneeling on the floor beside my bed. We were still at the hospital, but in an unfamiliar area—or building. I was in a recovery room of sorts. There were several other beds around me, each separated by a curtain. I was wrapped in gauze nearly from head to toe. I shifted to look around, but the pain was immense.

"Oh, Christ!" I saw a nurse at one of the other beds glance over at me.

"You're awake." Dane jumped up and pressed me back down.

"Were you just praying?" I narrowed my eyes at him.

"It's a Catholic hospital. It's encouraged."

I chuckled. "Ouch. How long was I out?"

"Twelve hours."

"Twelve! It's tomorrow morning? What happened?"

"You got ripped to shreds."

"Shreds?"

"They had you in surgery for three hours last night, cleaning your wounds and stitching you up." Dane rubbed his hands over his face and stood up. "I've never seen anything like that. Whatever is inside that room isn't a mischievous demon. It's something else entirely. It's something... evil. And that's saying a lot coming from me. I don't know what Paula was thinking sending you in there."

"Are you kidding? This was just another attempt at murder. Not technically by her hand, so it should stick."

"There is no way that thing qualifies as an innocent. She would have known that. Why would she risk it?"

"Have you seen her since I got out of there?"

"No, only the other one," he said with a certain bitterness in his tone.

"What did he have to say?"

"He came to gloat. Remind me that my ability to protect you was inadequate."

"It's okay, Dane. There's nothing else you could have done. I mean, for crying out loud, I had to pull in the wrath of God to save myself."

"Wrath of God?"

"Yeah, when I realized I wouldn't be able to protect myself, I sort of tapped into the coven. I may have used Rachel to fuel my escape."

"That explains the very irate phone call from her last night."

"What did she say?"

"She was in a rant about some sort of violation, but I didn't even give her a chance to get through it. I told her you were lying half-dead in a hospital bed and I didn't care what the fuck she was talking about and hung up on her."

"She's not wrong. It was a violation."

"And I still don't give a fuck. If you're alive right now because of what you did, then I'm glad you did it. We can deal with the fallout of that later. Right now, we just need to get you better. I'll see about getting you out of here."

CHAPTER 24

IT WASN'T AS DIFFICULT to get out of the hospital as I'd anticipated. There was a slew of paperwork for me to sign, declaring that I wouldn't hold the hospital liable for what happened to me, as well as any complications that might arise from leaving. In truth, I was certain they just wanted me out of there. As uncomfortable as they must have been with the 10-year-old time bomb in the south wing, they were just as uncomfortable with whatever had transpired in that room to cause my injuries.

Without a built-in line of morphine, I was feeling just how much damage the child had done to me. As I understood it, the wounds were mostly exterior, but collectively they were still life-threatening. Every step I took became anguish. The stitches in my legs went taut, threatening to rip apart the patchwork quilt that was now my skin.

The three steps leading up to my front door were enough to break a few sutures, so I settled in on the couch in the living room rather than head upstairs. Dane played the part of my nursemaid, fluffing my pillows and situating the coffee table within arm's reach so I could get to my water and the remote control, as needed. My intention had been to relax, but my mind kept drifting back to the battle—or perhaps I should call it a slaughter. There was something different about this possession. Not only the strength of the demon behind it, but in the power itself. I had felt it before. I had fought something similar. Something that made my fiery wrath seem like a tiny ember.

My mind eventually gave up trying to focus on a singular thought, and I drifted into a blissful, painless sleep.

Sometime later, minutes or hours, a loud slam drew me from my fitful dreams about rabid dogs. The sound of stomping feet further alarmed me, but my pain kept me from jumping up.

"Hennie!" Rachel's voice cut through the house. For a moment, my foggy mind thought she might've been there to check on me. To see if I was okay. "Where the hell are you?" she bellowed from upstairs. Soon after, I heard her footsteps clunk down the stairs as she rapidly descended.

"What are you doing here?" Dane asked her. His voice was coming from down the hall near the kitchen.

"Where is she?" Rachel asked, her voice dripping with ire. She was closer to me in the foyer, but I couldn't see her over the back of the couch, and she couldn't see me.

"She's in no condition for this."

"She should have thought about that before she took advantage of our connection."

"She needed it. She was in danger."

"She has plenty of power of her own. She doesn't need to steal from us."

"Her power wasn't working. She would've been killed if she didn't use you."

"I have no interest in hearing about whatever Hennie has gotten herself into. As far as I'm concerned, she is on her own."

"You really don't take any responsibility for her, do you?" Dane's footsteps came down the hall, stopping about halfway to the foyer.

"What are you talking about?"

"You don't get it," Dane scoffed. "She was normal before Sister Aggie brought her into this bullshit. You are the ones who capitalized on her power."

"That was before I realized where it was coming from."

"Power is power. It doesn't matter where it comes from."

"If that's true, then why did she need mine to protect herself?"

There was a pause, as if Dane was thinking about that himself. "I wonder, if you hadn't gotten your infusion, if you would've been a little more tolerant of Hennie's power."

"I don't pretend to understand Hennie, but I know she's dangerous."

"Is that what you do with dangerous people? You let them roam freely without any guidance or support?"

"It seems to be working well for you."

"You are such a hypocrite." Dane took a few more steps in her direction. "You and your coven created this entire situation. You brought me into this to protect you. You can't have it both ways. Either I'm the hero or I'm the heathen."

"Both ways? I don't have it *any* way. You may have been redeemed so you could protect us, but the only person you seem to have any loyalty to is Hennie."

"Is that what you want, Rachel? Do you want me to come back and protect you and your sisters?"

"That won't be necessary. Even if I wasn't capable of protecting myself now, all those nasty little shadows left with Hennie."

"You sure about that? I mean, hell, Paula was standing in your midst the entire time and you didn't even suspect."

"That was different."

"Why? Because it was the devil? That's what you really hate, isn't it? You were fooled twice. Once by a woman you considered your equal, and once by an underling. You can accept that Paula fooled you, but not Hennie. I bet it makes you sick to your stomach when you think of what she is and how you felt about her."

"I have no idea what you're talking about."

"Oh, yes, you do. You can put on the robe and you can ball that rosary up in your hands, but it doesn't change the way the pendulum swings. It didn't piss you off that I chose Hennie over you. It pissed you off that *she* chose *me* over you."

I heard a *thwack*, and I knew Rachel had slapped Dane. I stiffened despite the pain, in case I needed to jump up and protect her, but only silence followed. I could only imagine the silent but feral exchange transpiring between them, eyes glaring, lips snarling.

"I didn't come here to get into it with you, Dane," Rachel finally said. "I came here to make sure Hennie does not violate the sanctity of my coven again."

"If you're so concerned about the sanctity of your coven, then why don't you just extract her from it?"

"It's not that simple. We are intrinsically connected. I can't break the link."

"Then maybe it's time to stop ignoring her and start including her, because I don't imagine this shit is gonna get any easier from here on out."

"She can't just tap into it whenever she feels like it!"

"Even to save her life? Or have you become so addicted to your own power that you don't want to share it?"

"My power was meant to be used for good, not evil."

"Is that what you think she's been doing with it? She went to that hospital on Paula's orders." Dane's voice cut out, and he coughed. "She sent her to find—" Dane coughed again. "There's something evil there. Something that—" Dane coughed again, but this time he didn't stop.

"Are you okay?" Rachel asked when his breathing started to sound raspy. Dane let out a hacking cough and then gagged, as if he was vomiting. I heard Rachel gasp. "My God," she murmured.

I wasn't sure what was going on, but I knew there was no way I was going to stay on the couch and listen to him choke for another second. I ignored the pain and bolted upright. I stumbled around the sofa just as Rachel looked up at me from the foyer. The baffled look on her face turned angry, but as her eyes skirted over my bandaged body with streaks of red seeping in several areas, she frowned at me.

I rounded the wall that separated the hallway from the living room and saw Dane on all fours. His breathing was still raspy, but his coughing had turned into gargled choking sounds. There was something long and black coming out of his mouth. I wasn't sure what it was until I saw a similar black tendril on the floor beneath him. The baby snake writhed and twisted along the hardwood, searching for a hole to slither into.

I dropped to my knees and grabbed the head of the one still in his mouth and yanked it out. He was able to get in a decent breath, but it only brought another bout of coughing, which in turn brought on another round of gagging, and a new black critter appeared in his mouth. I reached in, struggling to grab the little tail that was whipping around like a secondary tongue.

"What's happening to him?" Rachel asked as she bent down to examine one of the snakes on the floor.

"I don't know. He was in that room with that thing, though. It must've affected him. It must've planted this in him." Knowing that I wasn't simply dealing with an infestation of snakes, but rather a magical incarnation, I reached for my power. I pushed my hand up against his chest, my fingers skirting his throat. I forced my will into the magic, demanding the aberration to cease.

As soon as my magic hit him, he convulsed. There was no more raspy breathing. There was only the compulsion of vomiting. His mouth opened wide and three more snakes joined the exodus. For a moment, he looked like a human squid with tentacles lashing out of his mouth.

I looked at Dane's bloodshot eyes above his bluish lips. He was no longer getting any breath. This was going to kill him, and my magic was only making it worse. He was going to die, and the thought of it made me ache deeper than I could have anticipated. I had been through tragedy after tragedy, death after death. I couldn't take any more of it. I couldn't lose Dane. He was all I had left.

I turned to Rachel. "I can't save him. My magic is useless against this thing. It's like fire against fire." My mind hitched on that thought, but I didn't have time to consider what I had figured out. I had to save Dane. "You're the only one who can help him. Your power, *His* power, will work."

Rachel looked from me to Dane. Then her eyes strayed away from both of us as if she was trying to refuse what her eyes were showing her. I sensed the struggle inside of her. She may have had sympathy for human life, but Dane's past made it easy to set that aside. His death could have been justified. Even if she still felt some connection to me, Dane may have been right about her resentment, whether it really was in regard to some sort of attraction or simply because she felt betrayed. Either way, killing Dane probably appealed to her heavily buried vengeful side.

As I watched her considering her decision, I felt something cool settle into my bones. My fear of losing Dane washed away, leaving something unfamiliar in its wake. My desire to maintain civility between Rachel and myself evaporated. As my anger rose, the power that usually tickled the tips of my fingers felt different. This was not my usual hell-fueled injection.

The exhilaration it provided was just as addictive, but it wasn't sensual or disorientating. It was the opposite. My physical body—including the pain from my wounds—disappeared entirely. It was as if my mind was the only functioning part of me. And deep in the amygdala, a thought was brewing. A consequence was being devised. A punishment was being prepared.

Before my power could grow that seed of retaliation, Rachel leaned down and pressed her hand against Dane's chest and back. Her eyelids flickered and her head rolled back to look at the ceiling. Dane released one final gushing torrent of snakes before taking in a deep breath.

As he gathered his bearings, he pressed his hand over Rachel's on his chest. He looked up at her as she quietly whispered her final extolment—a procedural thank-you card for services rendered.

Dane's gaze fluttered over her, partly exhausted and partly in awe. He wrapped his arms around her waist and pulled himself against her, burying his face in her bosom. Though the position was impertinent, he didn't appear to be doing it for any sexual purpose. He just wanted to be closer to her.

To my surprise, when Rachel came out of her semi-trance state, she didn't brush his arms off of her. She raised her hand to his head and petted him gently as if he were a child seeking affection from his mother. After a moment, Dane seemed to return to reality. He drew away from Rachel despondently. He cleared his throat and glanced at me, seemingly embarrassed or guilty. Rachel was otherwise unaffected by the moment. She must have accepted the burdens of being the middleman of adoration. She stood up and wiped away some of the drool Dane had left on her robe. She looked down at the snakes, now dead and shriveled on the floor. They had been real, not merely hallucinations. That in and of itself meant something, but I wasn't sure what.

"What was that?" Rachel asked me.

I wanted to give her an answer, but the truth was I didn't have one. Whatever was squatting inside that little girl in the hospital was not just another demon. It wasn't the standard possession of borrowed flesh.

It was something new.

CHAPTER 25

I LAY ON MY bed, being as still as possible, so I didn't disrupt Rachel's work. She had already healed my arms and the biggest gashes on my stomach, and now she was working on my legs. She carefully cut through the gauze wrapped around my left thigh. I had already broken the stitches on this one, so blood was pooling on the underside of the material, making it difficult to remove without pulling on the wound.

Despite the animosity that had been disintegrating our relationship, Rachel was being very gentle. There was a fresh bowl of warm water on my bedside table. Rachel dabbed the washcloth into it and moistened the gauze around my wounds to help release it. She looked over the deep cut and grimaced. She seemed to realize that my use of her power had not been unwarranted.

Before healing the gash, she swabbed away the excess blood around it and plucked out the stitches. She could heal me easier without encumbrance.

I looked over at Dane in the far corner of my room, sitting in a decorative armchair. Slouching back with one leg resting on his knee, his gaze had become hyper-focused on us. I had no doubt he was imagining several scenarios for the two of us. It wasn't difficult with me lying on the bed in only my bra and panties, and Rachel sitting on the bed carefully tending to my wounds, her hands only inches from *playing doctor* in a different way.

"I'm glad you tapped into my power." Rachel pressed her hand up against the gouge in my leg and I clamped my teeth together as the wound healed shut. It wouldn't be enough to restore me completely. The injuries would leave me with a few scars, but Rachel wouldn't waste the good stuff on me. Truthfully, I could have done it all myself, but given that I had just fallen off the wagon—down a steep cliff—it was probably best to let her do it. "You were nearly killed. Why did you even go in there?"

"Paula sent me in there."

"She did this to hurt you?"

"I did this so she couldn't deny the truth," Paula said from the doorway of my bedroom. We were all startled, but Dane jumped to his feet, ready for combat. He grabbed the woman by the arms and shoved her against the doorframe. "Easy now, Dane. I wouldn't want you to break your streak of good behavior."

"How dare you come here after what you did? Look what happened to her in there!"

Paula looked over his shoulder at Rachel and me. The corner of her mouth tipped up, and she perked an eyebrow at us. "Yes, this looks positively torturous."

"Let her go, Dane," Rachel said calmly. It surprised me that she, of all people, was maintaining her composure. Out of all of us, she had to be the one most disappointed in Paula's revealed identity. Even more surprising was that Dane released Paula without further coaching. He even walked away, giving the woman space to enter the room.

"Well, that was nice of you, Rachel," Paula said.

Rachel didn't look at her, she just continued to un-bandage the next wound that required her attention. "What is this truth that Hennie is not supposed to be denying?"

"The truth about her existence." Paula looked at me, leveling an unspoken accusation. We had gone round and round about how unnatural it was that I should exist to begin with, but of course the Big Guy had given me permission to stay in this body, so she could hardly argue the circumstances of my existence any longer. I was legitimately divorced from the devil, an independent being, until death do us join. Or something like that.

"You're going to have to give us a bit more information than that, Paula," Rachel said, maintaining her calm diplomatic voice.

"Okay, how about this?" Paula motioned to me. "Your little runaway stunt has screwed up the very fabric of the universe."

I stared at her for a moment. "Okay, so you're still pissed about me tattling on you to God and you wanted revenge. I thought the washing machine was my punishment for that."

"Washing machine?" Rachel looked between us.

"It's not my fault you were stupid enough to get into that mess."

"You were nearly drowned too!" I objected.

"I was caught off guard!" Paula defended.

"Ladies, does the washing machine really matter right now?" Rachel interrupted.

"No," Paula said. "What matters is that she is a plague on my very existence. Everything is falling apart because of her."

"Me! You're the one who tried to kill me *again*!"

"I didn't try to kill you. I warned you; fighting wouldn't do you any good. You were the one who decided you should try an exorcism."

"That's what I do!"

"No, it isn't!" Paula yelled. "Not anymore. Not since she kicked you out of the coven. Remember?"

The rebuttal on my tip of my tongue disintegrated. I looked at Rachel, but she wasn't paying attention to me, only to my wound.

Paula moved around the bed, forcing herself into Rachel's line of sight. "And why was that again, Rachel?" She didn't answer. "Why did you remove poor little Hennie from your life?"

"It was for the good of the coven."

"Oh, what a load of horseshit. You removed her because you didn't want to deal with her. Sister Aggie sensed what she was from the very beginning. That woman could sniff out trouble from a mile away. The difference between her and you? She embraced Hennie. Tried to mold her, train her."

"And look where that got her!" Rachel finally broke. She stood up and squared her shoulders. "She brought her into our group, bound us to her, and it destroyed us!" Rachel yelled across the mattress at Paula. I was glad she was standing up for herself, but I knew she was playing right into Paula's hand. "She thought she was saving her, and all she was doing was plugging us directly into hell!"

"You were always connected to hell." Paula motioned to herself.

"No, we were never connected to you. We were connected to some made-up version of yourself."

"Oh, we were connected more than you think. Didn't you wonder why it was so easy to share your secrets with me?"

"I thought it was because we were friends."

"We were never friends," Paula snapped, and my ears perked up.

"Believe me, I won't make that mistake—"

"Whoa!" I pulled myself up and raised my hands to stop both of them. "What the hell was that?" I looked at Paula. She narrowed her eyes at me. Rachel gave me a baffled look. "That was a lie." I pointed an accusing finger at Paula.

"What?" An intense snarl of confusion marred Paula's face, but I knew she understood my accusation.

"You just said you two were never friends." I waved a finger between them.

"We..." Paula's mouth contorted as she struggled to find a different way to say it that wouldn't catch her in a lie.

I draped my mouth open and laughed. "Holy crap! You actually enjoyed being Paula, the nun."

Paula started to shake her head, but stopped. Her jaw shifted as if trying to unhinge so she could swallow me alive to keep me from talking.

"I never understood why you stayed at the convent so long. Dedicated your mortal identity to playing a servant of God, especially when there was no real goal other than monitoring them."

"I was watching Sister Aggie."

"Oh, sure, at first, but she was untouchable. You stuck around because you liked being part of the coven."

"Don't be ridiculous!" Paula sneered. "Me enjoying the company of mankind is like befriending a zit!"

"If Tom Hanks can befriend a volleyball, the devil can certainly have some human pals."

"I will end you." Paula raised her hands, and I instantly felt a flood of power rise inside of me. It was hot and fast, making my pulse race. The sores on my arms re-opened, causing blood to pour out onto my sheets. With so little left to spare, I didn't have the strength to retaliate.

"No, you won't," I heard Rachel say behind me and a wave of new magic passed through me. It hit Paula like a rocket launcher in her gut. She flew back and crashed into my vanity, breaking the already blackened mirror. She slumped down, knocking powders and creams everywhere as she slipped to the floor, unconscious.

I also fell back, drained of any potential for movement. Rachel caught me against her and my head lolled back to look at her. She had a worried look on her face that made me happy. At least she cared if I lived or died.

"You are so much cooler than me," I mumbled and passed out.

Chapter 26

W E ALL SAT AT my dining room table listening to the grandfather clock tick in the hallway. My healing was complete, and I was capable of all sorts of conscious behaviors. I had showered away the excess blood and put on clean clothes for this part of the conversation. Dane was sitting at the head of the table, catty-corner from me. Paula had taken up a seat at the head on the other end. Rachel had taken a seat opposite me, but in the middle so she was neither next to, nor across from, anyone.

The three of us had reluctantly decided that there was still something that needed to be discussed and, in an effort to be civil, we agreed to sit down and talk. So far, however, the only exchange was of glares and silent threats. Dane's eyes hadn't left Paula, and she was keeping her silent fury on me. Rachel, on the other hand, was avoiding any and all eye contact with me. I wasn't even sure why she had stayed, but I supposed she had taken some interest in my revelation from earlier.

"Does anyone need a drink? Coffee? Soda?" I looked at Paula. "Goat's blood?"

Paula perked an eyebrow at me. "Funny."

"One of us has to be," I mumbled.

"What happened back there in the hospital?" Dane asked, getting us back on track.

Paula stared at him for a moment before answering. "That was the inevitable result of Hennie's independent state."

"I caused a possession?"

Paula scoffed and leaned back in her chair. "Don't think of it as a possession. Think of it as an assimilation."

I frowned and looked across the table at Rachel. She looked a little ill. Though, I wasn't sure if it was just the subject matter. "What is an assimilation?"

"It's when the possessor has full control of the body," Rachel answered. "What you faced today isn't supposed to exist. It's an aberration of nature, or rather, an abomination."

"So, like you?" I suggested to Paula.

Paula narrowed her eyes and twisted her jaw to prepare for a scathing retort, but Dane interrupted our banter once again.

"What happened in that room couldn't have been caused by a demon?"

Paula chuckled. "If only it were just a demon."

"What is it then?" I asked with a little more volume.

"You already know what it is. You just won't let yourself admit it."

I stared at Paula and shrugged. "No, I really don't."

"It's the beast." Rachel answered. I looked across the table at her. She stared off into space, not really looking at any of us. "I felt it the moment you connected with us. I have never experienced anything so..." Her voice trailed off.

"Enraged," I finished her sentence. The minute I said it, I realized she was right. My power was virtually useless against the creature in that room. That little girl absorbed everything I threw at her and rebounded it ten times over. I remembered fighting the beast one other time, but it had been restricted by the boundaries of an earthly plane. I couldn't imagine how much harder it would be to fight it on the same battlefield. Then again, I did know how much it would take. It would take the power of God—power I did not possess.

"How did this happen?" Dane asked. "You said Hennie was to blame. How did you mean that?"

"As we all know, we are in the middle of an unprecedented situation. When I created the trinity, I did so with the understanding that each component of my being would standalone for its singular purpose. In this form, I am human and I interact as a human. I observe, I manipulate, and when the occasion calls for it, I even indulge." Paula winked at Dane, but I didn't see an ounce of discomfort from him. In fact, of the three of us, he was the calmest.

"The beast was the epitome of my emotional consciousness. It was designed to be what man feared the most. It was my rage, my vengeance, and the designer of every man's punishment. It was meant to be an enforcer. My original self, my mind, and my soul, was always meant to be the control. When humans could not be manipulated or scared into doing my bidding, he would seduce them. Faith is rarely as strong as hunger or lust."

"So you had a nice little trifecta," Dane said. "Then Hennie got it in her head that she didn't want to be part of the trio anymore."

Paula groaned and shook her head. "Somewhere in the back of your mind, there's always a little voice that tells you what right and wrong are. Unfortunately, that little voice is relatively useless in my line of work. We pushed it away, as far away as we could. And then one day it just... snapped. My own conscience developed a conscience and ran away. It's absolutely ridiculous, but the fact of the matter is I was already split into thirds and then part of me broke away. I didn't have a way to compensate for that. Despite what all of you might think, the devil does actually need a conscience, a guide, not so much to assess right from wrong, but simply to draw a line in the sand."

"It was vital I get Hennie back. That she merge with my mind and heal the fracture. I knew the power would draw you in eventually. Unfortunately, I wasn't prepared for Daddy to interfere."

"Daddy?" Rachel asked.

Paula looked at her and tipped her head curiously. "Oh, don't tell me you don't know."

"Know what?" Rachel moved her gaze from Paula to me. Although I felt no shame for the blessing offered to me, I couldn't look Rachel in the eye. "What is she talking about?"

"Oh, this is wonderful," Paula purred with satisfaction. "You never told her. No wonder she dumped your ass. To think, all this time, she's been thinking of you as an abomination, just like me."

"Shut up, Paula. Hennie, tell me what she's talking about."

"I was given permission by God to maintain my soul—the devil's soul—in this body. I wasn't supposed to be here, but he gave me the go-ahead, at least until I die."

"How do you know God gave you permission?" A severe frown dragged down her lips. "Did he speak to you?" She asked it with an even tone, but I could tell she was already envious of even the suggestion that God would speak to me and not her. I was reluctant to tell her the truth since I didn't really have any proof of what happened. Her memories of the event were gone, including whatever transpired between her and the Big Guy upstairs.

"*You* told me."

"When?"

"Just before or after, I tried to commit suicide in the basement of the convent. Before the fire broke out."

Rachel stared at me, slack-jawed and searching my eyes for any hint of a lie. "I don't remember... How did I know about it?"

"He told you. God."

"God told me? He spoke to me? He told me to tell you that you have permission to be here, to use this body, to wield the power of Satan?" Rachel rose from her seat as she spoke. "He gave you permission to team up with this wretched piece of trash and embrace the dark side?"

This was going worse than I'd expected. "He told me I had to serve the devil, and he had to serve me. I didn't exactly have a guidebook for devils couple therapy, or in our case, quartet therapy."

"Do you have any idea how messed up that sounds? Why would He have anything to do with..." Rachel motioned broadly to me and Paula. "This?" she said disgustedly.

"I don't know. This makes about as much sense to me as it does to you."

"What else did I pass along from God? Did I give you any pointers on how to possess someone new when you get sick of this body?"

"No. You just told me you were sorry."

"Sorry for what?"

"For not being there for me during the hardest time in my life." It was my turn to rise from the chair. My heart was racing and my palms were sweating. I could feel a hint of the tingle in my fingertips, but it was nowhere near as strong as it had been when I'd thought she was going to abandon Dane.

"That's right," I said when Rachel's superiority faded. "You told me you loved me, but that you were about to be a shit friend. Good thing I got the apology upfront, cause God knows, I was never going to get it at the end." By this point in the conversation, my head was waggling with teenage attitude, but I didn't care. I had never really gotten the chance to be mad about Rachel's dismissal. I'd spent so much time being sad and mourning her loss that I never really embraced the concept of being mad at her. Which was strange, because I was usually really good at that part.

For a moment, Rachel only stared at me. Then, all at once, she looked around the table. "I can't be here. I can't be a part of this. I don't know what this is," she said to Paula, "but I want no part of it." Rachel turned back to me. "Don't trespass on our connection again, or I will be forced to expel you from our coven."

Rachel stepped away from the table and walked down the hall. I heard her grab her keys from the foyer table before slamming the door on her exit. She was gone, once again out of my life for who knows how long. Maybe it was forever this time. I wasn't even sure it mattered. It's not like we were actually friends anymore. Truthfully, I wasn't even sure we had been friends before.

"That went better than I expected," Paula said cheerfully. "A hell of a lot more entertaining, too."

"Can you just go, please?" I pleaded, not wanting to deal with her any more than I had to.

"We haven't finished talking about our problematic beastie."

"You deal with it. I can't even touch the damn thing."

"That's because your power and the beast's comes from the same place. Me, you, us. We can't fight ourselves. At best, we can hurt ourselves, but we can't win."

"Are you saying what I think you're saying?" Dane asked.

"I'm saying I can't fix this," Paula said. "The only person who can just walked out the door."

"You mean Rachel and the coven are the only ones who can fix this?" I asked.

"Yes." Paula shrugged, as if apologizing for the facts. "And you two are going to have to convince her to do it."

I looked back toward the front door, where Rachel had effectively stormed out. She wasn't likely to return willingly. She also wasn't likely to volunteer her coven to fix a problem that I had ultimately created. I couldn't even begin to imagine how I was going to get God's incumbent and the devil's embodiment to work together.

"Shit."

CHAPTER 27

I SAT AT THE folding table, rubbing my forehead. I already had a headache from three days of pleading with Rachel to help me with our runaway beast. She wasn't at liberty to deny me entrance to the church, but she had refused to take my calls. Any attempts I made to draw on our magical connection were met with a heavy-fisted repulsion spell. Now I had to deal with more of Paula's games.

The man across from me had lost his family to a drunk driver and wanted the devil's help to exact revenge against him. I rolled my eyes and looked at Paula. "Can we please stop doing this?"

"Can't you see this man is in pain?"

"No, he isn't. Do you know how I know? Because I can feel it. He isn't sad, he's mad. He should be sad, and if he would stop avoiding his pain, hc could possibly get on with the natural mourning process and forget about revenge plots."

"But the man was drunk!" my client pleaded louder.

I turned to the forty-something man with a heavy beard and beer belly. "So what?" I threw my hands up. "He was drinking, he fell asleep at the wheel, there was road construction, a deer, the weather, cell phones, and a fucking partridge in a pear tree!" I rose from my chair, power bristling on the tips of my fingers as the man's rage fueled my condescension. "They are dead!" He protested, but I interrupted. "THEY ARE DEAD!" I screamed at him. "And despite what you have built up in your mind, it was an accident. This man did not actively murder your family. He was convicted of the crime and sentenced accordingly. This path you are on is only a distraction that is quickly becoming an obsession. If you really want the man dead, then—"

"I don't want him dead," the man said eagerly. "I want his family dead. I want him to experience the same pain as me."

I frowned and turned to Paula. She was on the edge of her seat, watching me closely. Her predatory gaze was looking carnal in nature so I looked away.

"The answer is no," I said, leaving no room for negotiation. The man cussed me out before he faded into oblivion.

Paula jumped up and pressed her chest into my shoulder. "That was *wonderful*."

I drew my head back to get more space between our faces. "I said no."

"I know, but it was the way you said it. The disgust at his selfish human desire. For a fleeting moment, you sounded like... yourself again." She groaned and set her head on my shoulder. "Don't you miss being able to exert your power? To force others into submission?"

"No." I brushed her away and walked out of the back room.

"Don't lie to me, Hennie," she called after me as I walked along the bowling lane closest to the wall. "I know you enjoyed using your power against the beast. I could feel it."

"Then you should have also felt my frustration and guilt," I said as I pushed open the door to exit the bowling alley. As soon as I was outside, the sun bore down on me, clouding my vision for a moment as my eyes adjusted.

A hand grabbed my arm and spun me. My body was pressed into the brick wall of the building. For a fraction of a second, I saw horns and feral eyes before Paula's face emerged. She pressed her body against mine, and the wooden cross that hung from her uniform pressed into my hip.

"Those are the emotions of your human mind," she whispered. She raised her hand, and I flinched, but she only stroked a few hairs out of my face. "I know you think you can avoid this. I know you want to be away from us, but it is never going to happen. You belong to us."

A couple of men approached the door and looked over the scene. One was smiling, but the other man was grimacing. Something about a nun pressing up against another woman turned him off. His eyes landed on mine. I shook my head, answering his silent question. Even if I had wanted help, these men were no match for the devil, no matter what his form was.

"You're making a scene," I said after the men went inside.

"Do you think I give a shit about that? If I wanted to, I would strip you naked and fuck you right here in broad daylight for the whole world to see." The threat of a public rape should have scared me, but instead of cowering, I sputtered out a laugh. I snorted several times before I got my reaction under control. Her face contorted in outrage. "Do you think I'm lying?"

"No, I was just thinking you have nothing under that robe to fuck me with."

Her ire melted into a smug expression, and she took a step back. "Don't be so sure." She lowered her head and the air around her warbled like heat coming off a flame. I blinked several times before the image made sense again. The black robe had transformed into a black suit. The habit was now a layer of neatly gelled black hair. As *Paul* lifted his head, he rose to his full height. "Now," he said, voice deep with male bass. "What were you saying about me not being able to fuck you?"

I stared at him, still trying to understand the complex emotions that poured off of me when he was around. I was glad Paula had always appeared to me as a woman. Something about the mixture of my shadow and Paula's manipulative nature was too much. Rather than indulge in the disorienting temptation, I turned on my heel and started walking to my car. "I have no intention of humoring your semi-masturbatory fantasies."

Paul chuckled behind me; the deep resonance sounded maniacal. "I've been playing this all wrong, haven't I? This form is far more difficult for you to dismiss, isn't it?" He lengthened his stride and easily caught up to me. "I should have known. You do have a thing for bad boys."

I glanced over in time to see him wink at me. I stopped at my car door and turned to face him. "It doesn't matter what gender you are. You are not going to convince me to start using my power again. If you want to grant a man revenge, then do it. You have the same power I do." I opened the driver's side door, but he pressed his hand against it, slamming it shut. I barely got turned around before he pushed his body against mine. This time, it wasn't a wooden cross digging into my hip. I grunted at the almost painful pressure and bit my lip, so I didn't say anything that would piss him off.

"You still don't get it. You are my soul, my conscience. I can't decide to do *anything* without you."

My eyes flickered over his. "That's ridiculous. I don't control your actions."

His eyes narrowed. "Don't you?" He leaned in and kissed my neck. "I haven't made a move since you became aware of our connection." He moved up to my ear and whispered. "Normally, I see what I want and I take it, but I can't. Not unless you approve. Even if you aren't conscious of all the decisions you're making for us, you are making them." He suckled on my earlobe and I felt desire warm through me, down to my curling toes.

"That's why I need you, Hennie." His hands slipped around my thighs and lifted me. I gasped as he pressed himself against me, pinning me to the car. "We need to be as one. It's the only way to save us all." He rocked against me and I couldn't help imagining the potential union of our bodies. "Rachel is a stubborn woman—and selfish. I know you care for her, but she won't help you. The only choice we have left is to merge." Paul kissed me. His lips enveloped mine, and I tasted something metallic. He drew away, breathless, and looked at me. "I've always wondered what you would feel like pressed against me. Let me have you. All of you." He leaned back in to kiss me, and for a moment, the world spun. Before I knew it, spongy fabric hit my back and Paul pressed on top of me. The air was quiet and stale. I opened my eyes and realized he had put me down in the back seat of my car.

The moment was surreal. I felt arousal like nothing I had ever felt before, and I realized I was about to go through with it. I was going to let Paul fuck me in the parking lot of a bowling alley. How depressing was that?

Setting aside my feelings about public humping and the lack of romance, there was, of course, Dane. There was no way around it. I loved Dane. I shouldn't, and God knows why he loved me, but somehow we were both just screwed up enough to get along. I didn't want to cheat on him. Especially after I made such a big deal about him flirting with that girl at the hospital.

"Will you have me?" Paul spoke into my ear even as he undid my pants.

I panicked as the scene in my mind changed along with my desire. I wasn't even sure I *could* say no to him. He had already threatened to rape me. Did it matter if I said yes?

Then it hit me. That was his entire point. He needed me to make decisions for him.

I had never fully grasped the idea that I served the devil, and he served me. How could two people be in control of each other? I thought it was just a matter of partnership to share the power, but the power was his and the decision to use it was mine.

I tasted the blood in my mouth and Paul repeated his request for my body. What he was really asking was for permission to merge with me again. A contract had been laid down in front of me and I hadn't even known I was about to sign it.

"No," I answered, as his peppered kisses landed on the brim of my panties. He froze, and I felt the shift in his demeanor even before his horizontal pupils met mine. There was a darkness there even the beast couldn't compete with. Had I been merely human, I was certain he would have found countless ways to torture me for my disobedience. As it was, I wasn't certain he wouldn't try it anyway, disregarding the damage it would do to my shadow.

Fortunately, I didn't get a chance to find out before Paul was dragged out of the car by his heels.

CHAPTER 28

I SCOOTED OUT OF the car and zipped up my pants. I hadn't realized Dane had followed me to the bowling alley, though, once again, I wasn't sure why it should surprise me. He was perpetually hunting me down.

Dane threw Paul up against a nearby dumpster. With one hand twisted in his shirt, bracing him in place, his other hand punched Paul relentlessly. Blood showed on his face. His brow was cut, and his lip. "You keep your hands off her!" Dane snarled.

"I almost had her." Paul smiled, showing red teeth from the blood inside of his mouth. "There's something to this seduction thing, after all."

Dane roared and punched Paul in the stomach. He doubled over in pain and so did I. I caught sight of Paul as we both toppled to the ground. I heard him laugh, but the deep bass changed to a higher-pitched chortle. Paula lay on the ground laughing while Dane looked between her and the spot she had been standing.

My head ached and the blood I could taste in my mouth was now my own. "What happened?" I asked. There were very few hard and fast rules when it came to my other selves, but Paula and I didn't usually share pain.

Dane cussed and moved to me. I flinched as he reached under me to pick me up. "I'm sorry. He got in the way," he whispered.

Dane stowed me in the passenger-side seat and climbed into the driver's side. He peeled out of the parking lot at breakneck speed. I peeked over at him. I could see the anger that was forcing him to grip the steering wheel hard. I could also see the frustration he was feeling at not being able to exact his revenge.

"I'm sorry," I whispered to him.

He glanced over and frowned at the bruises that were no doubt blooming on my face. I hadn't felt the initial impact, but I was now feeling the effects of it. My shadow must have slipped into place over Paula. Their similar features would have made discerning the two very difficult. He played right into Paula's sick idea of a joke. "For what?" he asked.

"For letting him get that far."

"He was manipulating you," Dane defended.

"He shouldn't have gotten that far," I chastised my lack of self-control.

"No." Dane glanced at me again. "He shouldn't have." His jaw tensed.

"How much did you see?"

He didn't speak for a moment. He just stared out at the road, eyes glazed in concentration. "All of it," he finally admitted.

"Why didn't you break it up sooner?" I asked, a little hurt by his belated jealousy.

"I wanted to hear what your answer would be."

"I said no."

Dane nodded as he rolled his jaw. "Yes, you did... eventually."

Chapter 29

"**I**S PRIVACY EVER GOING to be possible for me?" I said, poking my head out of the shower to glare at Paula. She was sitting across the double-sink vanity in my upstairs bathroom, painting her nails black with my polish.

"I assumed after last week, you would be comfortable with me seeing you naked."

I popped my head out again and glared at her. "Don't do that. Don't pretend like your manipulation was some kind of bonding experience." I dove back under the shower spray to rinse out my conditioner.

"It would have been if Dane hadn't interrupted."

"I said 'no' long before that."

"Oh, please, you said 'no' to the soul binding. You still wanted the sex."

"Eew!" I reached out to grab my towel as Paula ripped back the curtain. I gritted my teeth and let her look me over. "See anything you want, or just wished you had?"

"Don't get too cocky, Hennie." Paula grabbed the towel off the hook and tossed it at me. "I know my male form has a good deal more influence on you than this one. There's a reason I haven't used it against you thus far."

"Oh?" I wrapped the towel tightly around me and grabbed another to dry my hair. "Why is that?"

"Because I need you to trust me more than I need you to lust for me."

"Well, it doesn't look like either is working for you." I pushed past her to get to the sink so I could brush out my snarls before they took hold.

Paula hopped up on the counter next to me and watched me put a random lock of my long hair into a tiny braid. "I know it's hard for you to understand what's happening." Her voice was soft with the lilt of her maternal self, the character I had grown accustomed to when I first met her. The woman I missed.

"It's hard for me, too. The world—your world—is built around a certain construct. Physics rules that can't be changed. But, of course, with magic, all those rules go out the window. Your power isn't acting against nature so much as nature is blocking others from doing it." She smirked. "We can't have humans running around randomly changing their gender and conjuring fire at will. That's a level of chaos even hell couldn't compete with."

I smiled at her dark humor. "Are you going somewhere with this?"

"I'm trying to tell you that the laws of nature are the spell and the spells are the real nature of the universe. When mistakes such as your inhabitation of a foreign body happen, it rips the spell. A little snag here and there is nothing that can't be healed, but your soul is still here, putting a deeper rent in the fabric of the human world the longer you stay. Now the beast has taken its cue from you and found itself a body. Another rip—a bigger rip."

"How was it able to do that? Don't I have some say in that as your conscience?"

"The beast is not a thinker. The beast, at best, can only be described as emotion. It was never meant to become a being. It was always just a source of vigor. The form is simply a result of human interpretation. The wild and angry presence translates to most as a predator, a lion."

I leaned against the sink and listening intently. As a nun in my coven, Paula had always sought to educate me. It was her honesty and ease with words that had made me trust her. Even though I knew she was nothing like that woman I'd known, there was still truth in the lessons and free-flowing knowledge was a trap I would never be able to escape.

"Does that mean you never had control of the beast?"

"In a way, yes." Paula picked up my brush and slipped off the counter. I ducked away from her when she brushed my hair. "It's all right. No tricks. I promise." I heard the truth in her words and I relaxed again. She drew the brush slowly through my long locks, being careful to untangle any knots before they tugged on my scalp. It felt wonderful and reminiscent of a time when I had a mother. The thought of my mother's death came back to me and I stepped away from her to face her.

"If you're trying to hurt me, you are succeeding," I admitted, tears forming in my eyes. Paula looked me over, perplexed. "How can you be so gentle and yet so conniving all at once?"

"I wasn't plotting anything. I'm sorry if I'm bringing up bad memories."

"You're bringing up *good* memories," I snapped and took the brush from her. "I hate that you exist," I said to her reflection. She averted her eyes and took a breath. "I hate that *I* exist," I whispered. "I never wanted any of this. Why couldn't you just leave me alone?"

"You know the answer to that. We waited long enough. Sister Aggie tried to protect you, but it was pointless. You always have and always will belong to us."

I stared at her reflection, feeling the futility of my fight. Whether it was today or in fifty years, I would eventually die. And when that happened, my proper vessel would automatically receive me.

Paula reached around me and grabbed the brush from my hand again. "I know what you're feeling." She moved slowly, drawing the brush up to the top of my head and down through my long locks. She paused a moment and looked at me through the mirror as if questioning whether she should continue. "I felt as you did once upon a time." When I didn't pull away from her, she continued to brush my hair.

"When I decided to split myself, it was meant to be an affront to God. It was a joke. However, when I first awakened as this body, as Paula, I felt alone. It was as if I had awakened from a coma. I knew where I had come from and I knew how I had come to be, but I had a new concept of self. I was a blank slate. The burden of anger had been lifted. For a long time, I had trouble reconciling my existence as a human with my past as an angel. I still longed for something of my own. Something separate from the others. Despite my best efforts, being human has certain requirements and necessities. Cravings far more urgent than food or pleasure."

"And what craving is that?"

"Companionship."

I sputtered out a laugh. I turned away from her grooming and leaned on the counter. "You can't possibly expect me to believe the devil requires human companionship."

Paula's eyes widened, and she tossed the brush into the sink. "What I require is to be entertained. I simply need others around me to manipulate. That is my purpose, after all."

I narrowed my eyes at her. "Is that why you befriended a group of witches?" Paula's eyes burrowed into mine, but she didn't answer, no doubt fearful I would detect her lie again. "What does it mean, Paula? What does it mean if the devil's human side gets attached? What happens if the devil finds love?"

"We're getting off topic, Hennie. We need to figure out what to do with the beast."

"I'm open to ideas. Rachel won't return my phone calls. She refuses to see me. How can I convince her to help us if she detests me?"

"Rachel is a simplistic creature. She harbors all the anger she always did, she just hides it under her veil. Much as she does all of her other personality traits. I think perhaps it's time we stop asking for her help."

"I don't think we can get violent with her. She kind of outranks me in the magic department."

"That may be true, but she doesn't outrank me. We'll do this together."

"Why do I get the feeling this is going to get very messy?"

Paula shrugged. "At the risk of being called a hero, I would remind you that short of bullying Rachel into doing this, we are doomed to live in a chaos on Earth, unbeknownst to hell. Perhaps we can chalk this up to the lesser of two evils."

"More like the lesser of four."

CHAPTER 30

THIS WAS NOT WHERE I wanted to be. I was supposed to be punishing evildoers. I was supposed to be balancing the rights and wrongs of humanity. That was the only good thing I could accomplish with the powers I siphoned from hell. Unfortunately, my task for the day was not against the morally objectionable portion of humanity. My duties involved crashing a party I had long since been kicked out of.

The convent had burned down nearly seven months ago, but the church was still in good condition. The early morning services only had a few truly devout Catholics or a few early risers with nothing better to do, so I had no concerns about disrupting the Mass. Among the devoted would be my former sisters, or all that remained of us after the devil had infiltrated us—infiltrated me.

I pushed through the heavy wood doors, making the hinges squawk. Out of habit, I dipped my fingers in the basin of holy water as I walked by. The water stung like lemon juice in an open sore, but I refused to be restricted. I pressed the acid into my forehead, ignoring the pain as I performed the sign of the cross.

The second set of doors I pushed open with the strength of my magic, partially to announce myself to my brethren and partially because it felt really cool. As the doors flew open, I smelled the undertone of incense that had long since embedded itself into the wood of the pews and its cushions. As little as I respected Catholicism as a hobby, I still felt at home here more than at my parents' house. My parents were dead, but my adoptive family was still alive and this was where they lived.

As I stepped from the narthex into the nave, I felt the air change. A thick wall blocked me and prevented me from pressing my foot to the floor. Or from any further forward movement. My heart thumped with the fear that God had finally cast me out of His house. Not just the warning of holy acid or hot rosary beads, but an outright blockade. Had God rejected me like my coven?

"Leave Hennie!" Rachel yelled down the aisle from the crossing.

I looked up and saw her standing at the head of her pack. They were all there—a neat row of witches disguised as nuns, each more powerful than the last time I had seen them. They were standing guard, ready for me. So much for a surprise attack.

"I'm not leaving until you agree to help us."

"I want nothing to do with your schemes. The work we do is for God and God alone."

"This isn't about God. This is about human existence. This is about righting a wrong."

"Who's wrong?" Rachel asked.

"It doesn't matter who's wrong it was. What's done is done and now we have to do something to prevent it from getting worse."

"I *am* preventing it from getting worse. I'm keeping my power as far away from you as I can."

"I'm not trying to hijack your power. I'm trying to recruit you. All of you. I need your help."

"Why would the devil need our help?" Meredith asked.

I wanted to clarify that *I* was the one asking for help, not the devil, but I was quite certain there was no distinction to them between me and my other three faces. Sooner or later, I was going to have to accept that myself. "There is a child at St. Mary's Hospital that needs to be..." I paused, wondering whether an exorcism would truly cut it. As Rachel had said, it was an assimilation, not a possession. I didn't know for sure, but I suspected this fight was going to be more arduous than the usual prayer circle. "I'm not sure what we need to do with her."

"You want our help for an exorcism?" Lynn asked. "Can't you just rip them out?"

I nodded and pushed my foot down to the floor. I reached for my power and sloughed off the minor spell that was keeping me from closing the distance to the sisters. There was a slight gasp as I did so, but Rachel didn't flinch. If she'd known I was coming, then she'd have known I had come with backup.

"If this were a normal possession, I would. I've gotten rather good at it, actually. But this isn't a normal possession. It's an assimilation." Katherine made the sign of the cross and clasped her hands around her rosary.

"Like Hennie," Rachel added.

I stared blankly at her for a moment. I hadn't much thought about myself as an assimilation, but clearly that was exactly what I was. I'd possessed a body, taking complete control of it. "Yes, like me."

"Tell them who it is," Rachel prompted.

I looked at her calm facade. She was playing the stoic matriarch very well, but I knew her. She was fuming inside. She wanted to wipe the floor with me, just to prove she could. So long as her righteousness held out, we could continue to converse civilly. "It's the beast," I said.

Katherine ducked behind Rachel, clasping her arms. "The beast has touched the Earth!"

"Settle down, Kate," Rachel admonished her and shrugged off her leeching grip. "This isn't our fight. That thing belongs to you. You let it out. You put it back in its cage."

"I can't. That thing is part of me and my power is useless against it."

"You're a clever girl. You'll figure it out."

"And if I don't? How many will get hurt? I agree in the end this is my fault, but who should suffer for that? Not innocents."

"The answer is no." Rachel waved her hand and my edging approach turned to a sliding reverse.

I growled as my feet slid back down the aisle and out the church doors. I flopped onto the steps outside, irritated that my grand cosmic power was just a slap in the face compared to what Rachel wielded.

I latched onto the deepest part of my power I could reach, snapping against the very ties that held me to the triad. The magic coursed in like a current of electricity.

"Careful, Hennie," my shadow said. I looked down and saw his face reflecting in a mud puddle. "Don't take more than your share."

"It's just a loan." I flicked the water, making his image warble.

I marched back up the steps. This time, the first set of doors flew open on their own, and the second set nearly broke off the hinges as they slammed open. I was vaguely aware that my stomping feet were now gliding. I was no longer walking, but floating toward the coven. They all cowered from my display, all except Rachel. Again, she was a freaking power-house, so she had nothing to fear from me.

I stopped midway down the aisle, leaving them space to breathe as I hovered over them. "I have tried asking you. I have tried begging you. I have even tried appealing to your compassion. So, I'm done asking. Help me... or else."

"Or else what?" Rachel tipped her head curiously. When I didn't give her an answer, she swatted her hand through the air. I subsequently went flying into a set of pews. I could feel the damage to my back, but I ignored it and threw much of the same treatment back at her.

I tried to aim for only Rachel, but the force of her backward launch sent her body colliding into Ruby and Meredith. All three landed just shy of the altar. As they stood up, I could see the anger and determination lighting their eyes.

Shit.

Ruby closed her hands together, and the entire church echoed with the squawk of shifting pews. The long wooden benches closed in around me, creating a barrier between them and me. I chuckled at the display. I swept my hands apart and the pews scattered even faster than they had arrived.

Meredith took her turn and stepped forward. "Down!" she commanded, and my legs collapsed beneath me. "Stay!" She snapped her fingers and my hands drew back behind me. Tethered to an imaginary pole, I couldn't move.

It was impressive.

But she still wasn't Rachel.

"Reverse!" I yelled, though it wasn't strictly necessary. I just wanted to stick to the theme.

Meredith and I instantly switched positions. She was now strapped to that imaginary pole and I was free. Now mere steps from Rachel, I turned to glare at her. "I can do this all day," I bragged.

Rachel started praying out loud. Her coven joined in with her. I rolled my eyes, but I was already feeling the heavy weight of air pressing down on me.

The voices crowded into my mind, a part of me, but separate—just like with the triad. I could feel each one of them. Their pain, their love, their desires, and even their hatred for me. They each had their own interpretation of me, but the general consensus was that I was no better than Paula.

Their combined power pressed me down to my hands and knees. I could feel the air leaving my lungs. They wouldn't kill me, to be sure, but they would knock me out and toss me back out the door.

I was livid, well beyond ephemeral irritation. I could once again feel that deep well inside of me that begged for vengeance. It was much darker than the human anger I usually felt. It was a place of bitterness. A place of retribution and inevitable ruination.

I wanted so badly to grab onto it. To shove that cold, sharp, raw energy down Rachel's throat, but I sensed it was a monumentally bad idea. The power was strong—stronger perhaps than this body could handle.

Whatever the case, I didn't truly want to hurt my sisters. They may have hated me, but I still loved them.

Instead of reaching for yet another unclean, addictive power, I grabbed onto them.

Despite my banishment, I remained linked to the coven like a dog on a leash. I had tapped into it out of desperation before, but now I did it out of anger. I absorbed the power Rachel was directing at me. Before she could adjust, I threw it back at them.

The witches scattered, thrown in all directions, like a bomb had gone off. Even pieces of the plaster walls cracked as the power impacted them. I kept hold of the connection afterward to monitor them, to make sure I hadn't hurt anyone seriously.

I heard a guttural cry and my body flew back. Rachel had already recovered and was charging toward me. I tasted blood and jumped up to face her. She cried out again, but this time I was ready for her. I deflected her attack, and the contrary power threw her back. "Will you stop this?" I yelled at her.

"Leave us alone!" Rachel threw the equivalent of a magical punch and I hit the floor again.

"I can't!" I croaked despite my shocked diaphragm. I dove behind a pew, narrowly avoiding another hit. "I'm trying to save the freaking world!" I peeked up to see if she had heard me, but had to duck right back down. The wood of the pew splintered, indicating that Rachel was not holding back her strength anymore.

"You are trying to destroy the human race!" she yelled back.

"Says who?"

"You infiltrated our group, just like Paula. You tricked us!"

"She tricked all of us! I have never lied to you!"

"I know what you've done. I know you've killed people."

I stood up from behind the pew, exposing myself to her attack. I no longer cared what havoc she reaped on my face. "So have you!" I stared back at her with an anger that matched her own. For a moment we both panted, plotting our next move or insult.

A slow clap broke our standoff. Rachel and the others looked back at the man sitting on the altar behind them. Paul was in fine form, as usual. The fine suit, the gelled hair, and the perfect beard. To me, he was simply the female version of Paula, but to them, he was a new player in this game. I was curious why she had chosen her male form, but I suspected she wanted everyone focused on the present and not the past.

Paul stopped clapping and slipped off the altar. "Have we had enough of the theatrics?" He adjusted his cufflinks before drawing his hands inward. The pews returned to their usual positions. I dropped onto the cushioned bench behind me and rode it back to the center aisle. I noticed the pew Rachel had damaged repaired itself, the splintered wood gathered back together in reverse. When Paul was done, there was no sign of a struggle anywhere—save my bloody lip.

"Who are you?" Meredith asked, looking Paul up and down as he passed her.

"I'm no one to fuck with, sweetheart," Paul said.

"How dare you enter the house of God, demon!" Ruby rasped at him.

Paul stopped and turned to her. "There are too many things wrong with that statement to correct. Your husband should've cut your tongue, not your lip."

I cringed at the taunt. It was a low blow. I shouldn't have expected him to pull his punches, but somehow I felt that the personal attacks were as childish as they were hurtful.

Rachel raised her hands to stop Paul's march down the aisle, but he just motioned downward, sending her to the floor. She lay there flat against the tile as he approached. "Listen, Rachel, I know Daddy gave you quite the arsenal, but it's a slingshot compared to what I have, so give it a rest." When he reached her, she leaned forward and kissed his shiny loafers. All the while, she seethed and groaned as if fighting her body with all her physical strength. "Are we done with the theatrics?"

"Yes!" I answered on Rachel's behalf. The others nodded.

He released Rachel from his dominance and she moved to stand. I rushed to her, offering her a hand up, but she just scoffed at me and moved back to stand with her coven. We all stood there, staring at Paul from opposite sides. There was more symbolism there than I could handle. I turned away to gather my emotions before I began to cry.

"All of you are under the mistaken impression that you can simply avoid this problem with the beast. You can't. This is not a good guy, bad guy situation. This isn't even a good guy, bad guy, worse guy situation." Paul motioned to Rachel, me, and himself, respectively. "This is a target, target, target..." Paul motioned to us all again, then pointed vaguely in the hospital's direction. "...fully loaded gun situation."

The women of the coven shifted uncomfortably, glancing at Rachel to see if this was true.

"I've explained this to Hennie, but I'll explain it to all of you, too. This situation isn't about fighting evil. It's about restoring the balance in the universe. That takes priority over our feud. It takes priority over everything."

"You can't force us to help. You aren't that powerful," Rachel pointed out.

"Do you really want the universe to unravel because you can't kiss and makeup with your ex?"

Rachel glanced at me. "We have been manipulated over and over again. How can we trust this is even real?"

"You saw it when I linked with you," I said. "You had to feel what I felt. That raw power. You said it yourself. That was the beast. It isn't meant to be a physical presence in this world. It's instinct without logic. It's pure wrath, and even if the fabric of the universe won't unravel with it being here, it can't stay. We have to send it back to hell—or at the very least, out of this form."

"I can't trust anything I see, feel, or touch from you."

My heart thumped hard against my chest. I took a breath, trying to remind myself that she had every right to doubt me. "Fine, then go see it yourself. Witness what it can do."

"You mean walk right into your trap?"

"Jesus Christ, Rachel! I don't want to hurt you! Can you at least trust that?"

Rachel paused a moment, but slowly shook her head.

"Fuck!" I turned around and stomped toward the exit.

"We aren't done," Paul called after me. I flipped him off over my shoulder. It would have been a nice tantrum to exit on, but he didn't let me go. I felt a tug on my body, from my neck down to the base of my spine. I turned around like a marionette doll and walked back down the aisle.

"What do you want me to do?" I asked Paul. "She doesn't trust me. We can't convince her of the danger. I don't know what else to do."

Paul turned to Rachel. "Then we must handle this as human enemies would. We must negotiate terms for our potential collaboration. What will it be? What will it take to start building a bridge between us once again—albeit a temporary one?"

Rachel glanced between us, then to her coven. She turned to Paul and raised her chin. "I'll go see your beast. I won't make any promises, but I'll evaluate the situation for myself—under one condition." She turned to look at me. "Hennie must be severed from our coven."

CHAPTER 31

I LOOKED AROUND THE old school turned convent, turned dilapidated mess of charred wood. I had never expected I would return to it. Certainly not to undo everything I had achieved there.

I could see the hole in the hall's floor where Dane had literally dug me out of the basement. The flames had started there and mostly devoured the main floor. They condemned the building for structural reasons, but the damage wasn't as bad as I expected. I could still make it to the stairs, which seemed sturdy enough, though each tread creaked disapprovingly at my weight. I glanced back at Dane, but he motioned for me to continue up on my own. If the stairs were grumbling at one body, they certainly wouldn't like the two of us together.

When I reached the second floor, I found Paula waiting for me. She glanced behind me where Dane's heavy weight was conjuring loud snaps from the wood. A final crack signaled something more severe, and I looked back in time to see Dane fall through the staircase.

I gasped and reached out as if it might be as easy as grabbing him. I pinched my eyes shut and waited for the inevitable sound of a crash, but it didn't come, only the clatter of wood fragments as they hit the floor on the main level.

I started to move back to the stairs to see what had happened when a hand grabbed my shoulder. I looked back and found Dane standing behind me beside Paula. I looked from him to her. She shrugged. "You gotta be quicker than that."

I considered thanking her for the gesture, though it may have had very little to do with me or Dane. Paula was eager to get this portion of the deal out of the way so we could be on to new business.

For the most part, the second floor had remained untouched by the fire. The damage was mainly from water and smoke. I looked at the library that housed more than a few sour memories for me. The glass windows were either broken or covered with soot. Dane took my hand in his and tugged me down the hall where Rachel was waiting for us outside of one of the old classrooms.

"Nothing like coming home again," Paula said as she sauntered down the hall toward Rachel.

Rachel shook her head. "This was never your home. Your home is in hell."

Paula stopped beside her and looked her up and down. Rachel waited for her snide remark, her clever jab, but it never came. Paula turned on her heel and went into the classroom. I wondered if any of what Paula had said to me the other night was true. It wasn't a lie, of course, but the degree of emotion behind it was subjective. Had she really enjoyed the companionship of humans? Had her human side seeped in just a little too deep? That, of course, was always the devil's downfall—being a little too human. I couldn't imagine the conflict inside of Paula was any less confusing than what I was going through.

When I reached the door to the classroom, Dane released my hand and ushered me inside. "Give me a moment. Rachel and I have something to discuss."

I didn't like the sound of that. I also didn't like that Dane reached past me and pulled the door shut between us. I stared out at the two of them through the glass, questioning the motivation for anything private between them.

I looked over the faces of the women sitting in a circle in the middle of the classroom floor. A wave of déjà vu flooded my senses. It was right in this room that I'd intended to murder my soon-to-be mentor. It was here that my sisters tore down my emotional barriers and brought me into the fold of their coven. It was here that I'd discovered my powers.

Several uneasy faces looked back at me. I was certain they would've been happy to never see me again, but I didn't have that luxury. I wasn't sure I had ever been destined for a hero's journey, but I was certain the destruction of reality was going a little too far, even for a villain. Except maybe the beast, but it wasn't the smartest of this triad. It was just the meanest.

Paula approached me and leaned in to whisper in my ear. "Would you like to hear what they're saying?" Before I could answer "yes" or "no," Dane's voice sounded in my ears.

"That's just it, Rachel. You aren't protecting anyone. This is only going to drive her further into his control."

"She is already under his control."

"No, *she* has control. She's able to resist using the power."

"And what was that yesterday? She wasn't exactly tossing a Ouija board and tarot cards at me."

"As I understand it, you weren't exactly tossing softballs at her either. You could've killed her."

"What do you want me to do, Dane? I'm already going against all of my instincts to help the two women in my life who have cut me the deepest."

"I know this is hard for you. I know you're still adapting to being the leader, but if you remove her connection to you, then you remove her last connection to God. All that's left after that... is him."

"Don't you understand this? As long as we are connected to her, we are also connected to him. We can't continue to operate as a force of good while one of our ranks is dripping with power outsourced by the devil."

"You are stronger with her than without her."

"I'm doing just fine, thank you. If I wanted to consult with a serial murderer, I would have let you know." I could hear the knob to the door twist.

"It's always interesting to see how power affects people," Dane said.

The knob creaked as it returned to its original position. "What is that supposed to mean?"

"It means that when Sister Aggie was in charge, she brought Hennie in under her wing. She tried to protect her from all of this. She tried to guide her, even though it put all of you at risk. You, on the other hand, have abandoned her, exiled her, and now, when she is on the precipice of losing everything, you are actively participating in her demise."

"I'm the bad guy now?"

"Fuck the good guy, bad guy routine, Rachel! Quit trying to be mother superior and start acting like yourself."

"And just who do you think I am?"

"You're somebody who has been through a lot of shit in your life and I think you know people aren't black and white. There is a difference between somebody who is caught in an impossible situation and somebody who means to do you harm. Hennie is caught in an impossible situation, and she is trying to make the best of it. So what the hell are *you* doing?"

The door pushed open, and Dane entered the room. I looked away, feeling guilty for my eavesdropping, but encouraged by his stalwart support. As Rachel came in, we caught each other's eye. She held my gaze for a second or two before looking away again. "Let's get started," she announced and headed over to join the circle.

Chapter 32

My sisters ripped away from me. Thread by thread, the ties that bound me to the coven unraveled. It wasn't about the power. It was about the stability. It felt like the very foundation of my mind was going with them. And they couldn't have cared less.

Their indifference to my pain made me feel as if I had lost my father all over again. I was alone and angry then. The bitterness of life had steered me toward the wrong answers. Suicide, murder, destruction in any form. The desire to have control over something in my life.

Tears poured down my cheeks as I looked at Rachel. She was now the pinnacle of goodness, a representative of God's will. However, looking at her in that moment, I couldn't see anything beyond her betrayal.

It was true I was part of the devil, but I had no choice in that. I had been lied to and manipulated as much as she had. I had been reborn and awakened with a clean slate. But her... She was willfully turning her back on me. Even after God himself had given me permission to remain on Earth, she was doing her damnedest to put me back into hell. Dane was right. Her power had corrupted her just as much as mine had me. I thirsted for vengeance, and she thirsted for justice.

But this wasn't justice. This was a bitch slap. This was her lording her own power over mine. Dominating me. Cowing me into being weak.

As the last tendril of the coven snapped, I felt something inside of me unfurl. The deep, raw core inside of me awakened, as it had when I'd thought Rachel was going to let Dane die. It seemed to feed on the bitterness that her betrayals inspired. With my addictions under control and no coven to latch onto, I didn't know how to tamp out its expanding grip.

Soothing veins of icy hot poured over my body. I could feel it trickle into my extremities. When the burn hit my already attentive brain, the anger and sadness I was feeling disappeared. My tears stopped instantly, and I looked up at Rachel with a detached clarity.

"No, Hennie," Paula whispered from the circle's edge. Though she was technically still part of the coven, Rachel insisted she not take part. Since Paula was trying to be diplomatic—for a change—she had agreed. I knew Rachel would have preferred to banish her from the coven right along with me, but without Paula's permission, it would be a nearly impossible feat.

I directed my mounting questions at Paula, seeking answers for what I was feeling—what I had uncovered.

"Let it go," Paula commanded as if I were a dog holding onto a chew toy.

I didn't let it go, though. This energy was new. It was something different. I didn't feel drugged. I didn't feel an underlying carnal desire. I felt at ease, calm, and very strong.

My senses were alive in a way I couldn't describe. Nothing was different and yet everything was different. It felt like...

I opened my mouth and let out a long breath I had been holding and turned to face Rachel. She was looking at me with wide eyes now. I was no longer part of the coven, but she could no doubt sense the power emanating from me like static electricity.

A droning sound filled the room, and the coven looked at each other, fear wiping away their disregard for me.

Rachel raised her hands, palms forward. I felt a pressure settle in around me. It was immense, as if the whole of the world was pressing on my shoulders, but it didn't hurt me. Nothing hurt. I wasn't even sure I could feel my body—and yet I felt everything.

"Everyone out!" Rachel yelled. Her fellow witches didn't need a second to consider the option of escape. They leaped to their feet and ran out of the room.

Dane, on the other hand, came closer to me. He watched me from the edge of the original circle like a man looking into an aquarium. "What's happening to her?" he asked loudly to be heard over the increased pitch of the droning noise.

"A side effect of her release," Paula called back to him.

"You knew this would happen, didn't you?" Rachel snapped at her.

"I suspected it could," Paula yelled.

"This was all a trick, wasn't it? What have we done?" Rachel yelled back.

It took until then for me to realize that the now piercing sound filling the room was coming from me. My mouth was open, and I was emitting an awful screeching sound, as if I had swallowed a wild banshee whole. The noise was unsettling, but I couldn't seem to stop it.

What the hell was happening to me?

"The coven was tempering her power. Now that the connection is broken, she is bearing the full weight of it."

"So rein it back in!" Rachel yelled at her.

"I can't. I'm not what's fueling this."

"What is?" Dane asked.

"Her soul. My soul. Our soul. She's tapped into her origin power."

"Enough of this bullshit!" Rachel pulled something from beneath her robe and threw it at me. I reached out and grabbed it even before I knew what I was doing.

I dropped my eyes to the dagger in my hand, the blade just inches from my heart—in more ways than one. I couldn't believe it. She had tried to kill me.

"Rachel, you idiot. Don't antagonize her!" Paula sniped. "Hennie, listen to me." Paula came into my view, but I didn't take my eyes off Rachel. "This is too much. You'll only make yourself ill again if you keep hold of it. Let it go and the pain will go away."

I finally turned to look at Paula. The screech in my throat died, and I spoke. "There is no pain." Her eyes flickered over mine, searching me for the truth, but I wasn't lying. Nothing about this power felt wrong. Nothing about it felt contaminated. It felt natural.

I threw the knife back at Rachel. Before it reached her, the metal shattered into a thousand tiny splinters. Each sliver embedded itself into her bare skin, making her hiss and bleed. Rachel leaped to her feet and so did I.

"Don't do this, Hennie," my shadow spoke to me from the reflection in the schoolhouse window. I could see him come in close behind me through the reflection. He wrapped his arms around me. "Push it down." I felt his power surge, pressing against me. He was trying to insert himself inside of me. He was using the full armada of euphoria to tempt me back into my drug-addled state of dependency, but I was beyond bodily pleasures at the moment. I felt... transcendent.

"No!" I reached out and grabbed Rachel with my magic. She winced at the pressure I put on her. She tried to fight back, but her power withered even as it reached me. She turned red as my grip robbed her of her ability to breathe.

Paula put herself in front of me, cupping my shoulders in her palms. She closed her eyes and more power pushed into me. Both Paula and my shadow intoned—a rhythmic foreign language that turned into the hardened garbled speech of a satanic chant.

I fought against it. I wanted this power. This was so much better than what hell provided. Clean and pure.

Paula changed to Paul before me. His dark beauty, ever alluring to me, shattered my focus. He bent down and kissed me. Energy sheeted off him, penetrating any weakness in my offense. My thoughts spiraled as I started to feel human again. His tongue pressed between my lips, disrupting my concentration altogether. I lost grip on the power and I released Rachel.

My legs gave out and Paul caught me in an embrace. My head lolled off his shoulder as I completely gave in to the rush of pleasure that was surging through me.

Half-drunk, half-dizzy, and half-high, I looked at Rachel coughing on the floor. She should have been afraid of me, but her eyes were glittering with a feral determination.

I wondered what Dane thought of this new display, but he wasn't afraid either. He looked disappointed. I assumed it wasn't easy for him to see me making out with Paul again, but I sensed his disappointment went deeper than that.

As necessary as it may have been, I had succumbed to the power of hell once again. I was weak. I was an addict.

CHAPTER 33

WE SAT IN THE old office—which had plenty of fire damage on the walls and water damage on the desk and chairs, but, again, was structurally sound enough to support a short meeting.

Paula now sat beside me, while Rachel took the head chair. Whatever irony there was in the switch was not amusing to me.

"You expect me to help you after the shit you just pulled?" Rachel rasped. She was still recovering from my attack. An attack that had technically been self-defense—or at least quid pro quo.

"I didn't pull anything. This was your fault," Paula insisted. "You can't pull on strings and expect everything to stay together. Hennie's powers were developed while being linked to your coven. She is used to threading the extent of it through a natural set of dampeners. You just took the dampeners away. Not only that, but you broke *our* link in the process."

"What do mean?" Rachel asked.

"I mean you... You effectively pulled off a scab. For a moment, she had no protection. She was openly bleeding. I had to..." Paula threw up her arms. "...make her clot again."

"That's a lovely metaphor, but what does it mean? What was bleeding?"

"Her soul."

"The devil's soul?" Rachel asked.

"Yes. The source of our existence. Our origin."

"You're talking about angelic power?"

"No. Angels, humans, dogs. It's all just the body. Her power is the raw building blocks of nature. The fuel of life. The problem is, while humans have a nice little flame in their soul, Hennie has jet fuel. She was never meant to discover it. She was never meant to use it."

"Why not?" I asked.

"Because jet fuel and humans don't mix."

"It felt good though," I said. "It didn't hurt."

"Neither did my power at first," Paula snapped. "Ignorant children, both of you. You are playing with magic that is well beyond your comprehension. You at least have God to watch over you. But you..." Paula pointed a finger at me. "Can't you see how this is all building to disaster? Do you really think the world can survive this many attacks on the fabric of reality? You are a walking, talking hole punch.

"I know neither one of you trusts me. But if we are going to get through this, if we are going to do anything to prevent hell on earth, then you need to start trusting each other. You can sort out your feelings later, because right now the beast's reach is growing. It is pushing the boundaries of nature aside and creating its own hell right smack dab in the middle of a Catholic hospital. And believe it or not, the three of us are the only ones who can stop it.

"So put aside your rosary and your pride." Paula looked at Rachel. "And you put aside your sour grapes." Paula looked at me. "Because you are going to be working together."

"I haven't agreed to do anything yet," Rachel said.

"You will," Paula assured her. "Once you see what's inside that hospital, lying in that bed, you will break vows and bones to be rid of it." Paula turned on her heel and walked out.

I stood to leave, but froze. I mustered up the very littlest of courage and turned to Rachel. She stiffened, which annoyed me, but it was understandable. "I'm sorry I tried to kill you. I wasn't thinking straight."

Rachel stared at me as I waited for her half of the apology. She shook her head slightly. "I won't apologize for defending the world from the devil. If things are as bad as she says, then we may have to work together, but don't think for one second this is over between us. As far as I am concerned, you don't belong in that body—"

"God granted me permission."

"Says you. I have no memory of that conversation."

"I'm not lying," I insisted.

"I have no way of knowing for sure."

"Fine. If that's the way it has to be, then so be it. But know this." I leaned over the desk, making her stiffen again. "I was holding back up there... a lot." I narrowed my eyes. "Do you think I'm lying?" I smirked a little before storming out of the office.

CHAPTER 34

"**S**HIT," I HISSED AS I stopped in the hospital entryway. Since we had left, there had been a shift in the way it looked. It had always appeared outmoded in design and décor before, but now the pastel green looked more sickly than before. The lights seemed dimmer. The occasional fluorescent bulb flickered, casting unnatural shadows against the walls.

I hoped the thick feeling in the air was because of a broken steam pipe, but my hopes were dashed when Paula stepped up beside me, looking over the area with the same worry pinching her brow. "It's getting stronger," she said.

"It was strong to start with. How much stronger can it get?"

Paula looked at me for a moment before looking away, leaving my question unanswered.

Rachel came up on my right. She glanced over the area, then turned to me. Her eyes flickered over my face. "I don't suppose we can stop here and call it a day?" I asked.

"One spooky room isn't proof of your claim," she said. "I won't be tricked into being your puppet."

I scoffed. "The last time I was here, the beast played plenty of tricks on me. It was difficult to discern my reality from its fiction."

"Reality no longer exists here." Paula turned back to the remainder of the coven. "The rest of you should stay here. We'll need help to get back if things should go badly."

"What do you mean, badly?" Meredith asked. "You aren't going to go after that thing without us."

"No, of course not," Paula said. "We'll need every one of you to defeat it. Which is why it's best to keep you out of harm's way until the time comes. You too, Dane."

"I'm not leaving Hennie's side." Dane stepped forward, pressing into my back.

"As noble and romantic as that is, I think you'll find you have nothing to offer her that I can't." Paula's face and body shifted into Paul. I immediately noted the smell of aftershave and ash. "Don't worry, I'll keep her safe." Paul raised his hand, caressing down my cheek. I batted him away and stepped free of the stare-down going on between the two men.

"Can we get this over with?"

"Please," Rachel agreed, following me to the stairs.

As we climbed to the color change of peach, I noticed Dane trailing behind Paul to the steps. For a moment, I thought he was going to disregard his order and come with us anyway, but instead he veered off to the front desk and greeted the busty redhead that had taken a shine to him the last time we were there. He immediately brandished his broad smile, gaining her attention right away. As she leaned over the counter to flash her own demure smile, his sly eyes shifted upward to make sure I was seeing the display.

Fair was fair. The last week had been a challenge on his nerves and heartstrings, but I hated that he was rubbing my nose in it. My attraction to Paul was not truly within my power to control.

"Stay focused," Paula said as she passed by me.

I frowned at Dane and jogged up the stairs to catch up with Paula. "Would you stop changing gender? It's really confusing."

"Rachel, don't get too far ahead," Paula said. "We should stick together."

Rachel glanced back at us, but otherwise continued her pace down into the yellow section.

"She doesn't trust us. She still thinks we're plotting something," I said.

"Trust is not her strong suit," Paula said, matching stride with mine. "I'm quite certain the only people she ever trusted were Sister Aggie and me." Paula grimaced at me. "Look how that turned out."

"Yeah, you forced her to kill Aggie."

Paula snorted. "Sister Aggie was dead the minute she swallowed up those demons. A noble sacrifice, but a sacrifice it was."

"How can you speak so blithely about her demise? Wasn't she your friend as well?"

Paula didn't answer at first. I thought perhaps she didn't want to get caught in a lie. "No, I think Aggie always suspected something of me. She was a very smart woman. If I didn't know any better, I would say she invited me into the group *because* she suspected me."

"Why would she do that?"

"For the same reason, she invited you. She thought she could save me. Diminish the evil inside of me. Find some sliver of good in me. Or perhaps God told her to."

"Why would God want you to be part of a coven—especially a faith-based one?"

"Haven't you heard? God works in mysterious ways."

"That's an excuse to rationalize the stupid shit in life. Seriously, why would your creator support your schemes?"

"For the reasons I just said. He still thinks there is good inside of me."

"Is there? A sliver at least?"

Paula stopped and looked at me. A small smile curved her lips as she looked me over. "You would like that, wouldn't you?"

"I would like it to not all be an act. I would like to see some of the humanity that spoiled the devil for heaven."

"And how would you have me express that humanity? What gesture would satisfy your craving for my benevolence?"

I swallowed hard. "Let me go." I paused, waiting for her to laugh in my face, but she didn't. "Let me live out the remainder of my life in peace."

"Mmm." Paula raised her hand and stroked my face. "If only it were so simple. You see, there *is* a sliver of good left in me. You." She poked my nose. "And I can't be a good guy without you." She shrugged. "So, you see, you can't have it both ways. This situation with the beast is only further proof that our current dispensation isn't going to work anymore. Once the beast is back in place. It's your turn."

I turned to walk away, but she grabbed my arm and pulled me back. In the short span between turning away and coming back, she had changed to Paul. "We will be together, Hennie. One body, one mind, one soul."

"And one angry chip on our shoulder." I ripped my arm free and continued down the yellow hallway.

CHAPTER 35

"Rachel," I called out to her, but she had no intention of slowing down. If I hadn't known any better, I would have assumed she was dead set on seeing the beast. She was either far braver than me, or she couldn't feel the evil rippling off this place like the others could.

The normally mild nurses roaming the halls were constantly looking behind them as if checking for danger. One was so startled by us walking by that she dropped a tray of food.

"Do you think they can sense what we are?" I asked when the clumsy nurse didn't readily take her eyes off Paula.

"The veil that normally blinds humans is starting to fall. She may well be seeing more than she should." Paula glanced back, and the girl yelped and ran away. "Hmm, that's not good."

"Maybe you should hide your face."

"Not her, them." Paula pointed forward down the hall where a line of cloaked figures was standing before Rachel. She had stopped in front of them.

"Oh, God, who are they?" I asked. "Please tell me they aren't devil worshipers."

"You can see them?" Paula asked.

"Yeah, of course."

"Those aren't humans, Hennie."

I looked at them again. It was more evident on my second inspection that they had no feet, or hands, or discernible faces. The cloaks were all I could see of them. "Demons?" I guessed.

Rachel began moving again, passing right through the wispy black smoke that created the cloaks. Once she was through, the smoke coalesced again, looking solid and tangible.

I followed Paula forward, despite my desire to turn back. Up until then, the power thrumming through the building had felt normal to me. It was feral, but far from frightening. To me, it was almost enticing. However, these demons were different from me. They felt... dangerous.

The long trill of a flat-lined heart monitor drew my attention from one of the rooms we were passing. I looked inside to see who had left this world. An old man, dosed into a stupor, was finally succumbing to his end.

The nun sitting at his bedside, back to me, reached to his chest—through his chest. I stopped and gravitated toward the scene. Out of his chest, she drew a glowing orb. All at once, I realized the robe I'd thought I was seeing was actually a cloak. "Leave him alone, you bastard!" I yelled at the demon.

The head of the cloak slowly turned to look at me. At first, there was nothing but black, but then a few vague features emerged in the black smoke.

"What are you doing?" Paula whispered to me.

I looked back and saw her on her knee, genuflecting. "Why are you—?" I felt a breeze of stinging cold air. I turned back and saw the demon right on top of me. Six, seven, ten feet tall—it didn't matter. It was looming over me, the smoky head reflecting my face back at me, along with a glimmer of a skull somewhere deep in the hood.

"That's not a demon, Hennie!" Paula rasped. "If you don't want to die, then I suggest you show some goddamn respect."

Death?

Or at least a minion of Death. I glanced down the hall and noticed the cloaked figures were paying attention to me. Monitoring the situation.

I knew what happened when you pissed off the devil, but what happened when you pissed off Death? The answer seemed pretty obvious, but there was no sense in finding out for certain.

I followed Paula's lead and, heeding the advice of Jane Goodall, I lowered myself to the ground, tucked my head and averted my eyes. I was not worthy. I was not his equal. I was gum on his shoes.

I felt another swift breeze, and the cloaked figure was gone. His exit immediately brought relief to my muscles. I even laughed, somehow elated by the unnerving experience. I looked back at Paula, who was scolding me with her eyes. I smirked at her. "So that's what a brush with Death feels like."

CHAPTER 36

"HE'S LIKE THE BEAST, isn't he?" I asked as we turned down the L-section in the hall. The path was getting unnaturally dark and cold, but I had long since lost a visual on Rachel, so I quickened my pace, ignoring the visual cues to *"turn back before it's too late."*

"Who?"

"Death. I mean, he isn't really a being. More like an idea come to life."

"Yes, I suppose there are similarities. Except the beast is a part of me. Just as you are. Death is independent of a consciousness. Not even God can control him."

"Seriously?" I asked.

"People like to believe God controls when they live or die. That's why they take risks so freely. They believe when it's their time, something or someone will kill them, so it's completely out of their hands. The reality is stupid decisions and mistakes can take you at any time. And Death will collect you as he always does."

"That's a little depressing."

"Yes, it is." Paula slowed to a stop.

I looked back at her and motioned to the double doors. "Come on, let's go. Rachel is already inside."

Paula narrowed her eyes at the doors. "I think it's best if I don't go in with you."

"What? Why?"

"The beast has a far stronger connection to me than you. I would hate to become... distracted from our goal."

"But what if something happens?" I asked.

"Then Rachel will get an opportunity to show off."

"And if it's too much for her?"

"Then another will take her place. They always do."

"What does that mean?" Paula walked off before answering me. "Why did you even come this far?" I yelled after her. "Chicken shit," I mumbled to myself, and pushed through the doors.

As I passed through to the next section, I was met with bright lighting reflecting off starch white walls and a polished tile floor. The ancient hospital was gone—or rather, transformed into its original luster.

A pair of women walked down the hall together, shoes squeaking and pantyhose scraping as they whispered the latest gossip to each other. I recognized the old-style uniforms and unnecessary pointy hats of the nurse's profession. However, it wasn't Halloween, and these weren't costumes. They took one look at me and stopped. "Can we help you with something?"

"I'm looking for a little girl. About yea high." I motioned to the height of my shoulder. "Inhabited by the incarnation of the devil's moodiness."

The women frowned at me. "Check the coma ward. That's the only child here," one of them answered.

They walked on, through the swinging doors. Out of pure curiosity, I moved back and pushed the doors open.

The other side was the same as before—dark, dank, and with no sign of the pleasant nurses.

"Great. Either I'm seeing ghosts or I've stepped through a time warp."

I headed into the so-called coma ward, the same place I had found the girl the last time. Much as the hall leading to it, the room was bright, without decay, and in working order. Or at least working order for the 1950s. The equipment that had previously been piled in the corners of the room was now fully functional. Ventilators sat beside most of the beds. Glass bottle IV drips hung above the patients. Beyond that, there were no beeps and bleeps.

At the far end of the room was a little girl, sleeping in her bed—seemingly unconscious.

"Is this what you're afraid of?" Rachel came up behind me. "A little girl asleep in her bed."

"That's not a little girl." I poked my finger at her.

"It *is* a little girl. She's sick. She needs medical care, not an exorcism."

"Then how do you explain this? Unless you have the power to travel through time, this isn't right."

Rachel looked around the room, as if seeing it for the first time. "We can't do anything for her. She's already gone. She'll die if we try to remove it."

"I don't think that matters."

"Doesn't matter?" Rachel frowned at me. "That's a human life. She's not dispensable."

"Under normal circumstances, no, of course not, but this is bigger than her. We have to—I don't know—save the world. Isn't that why the coven was started? To protect the world from the influence of Satan? I would say this is a pretty big influencer."

"And what if you're wrong?" she asked.

"What do you mean?"

"What if this isn't what we think it is?"

"It's the big bad wolf, only this time he's dressed up as Little Red Riding Hood."

"Hennie, I know you want to see the good in people. You see the good in me. You see the good in Dane. You even see the good in Paula. It's admirable, but it's naïve. This child isn't possessed. She's bait."

"Bait?"

"You're playing right into her hands, diving right back into your power addiction. Paula wants you and me in this room, putting everything we've got at it. And when we fail, she will show her true cards. She's using you to get me here. And when the time comes, she'll use me to get to you."

I blinked, not sure how to respond to that. "Even if that's true, the beast is still—"

"A figment of your imagination. Tell me this: did you actually see the girl attack you?"

"I don't know. So much was happening. I couldn't tell up from down. I just knew I was in pain."

"So you called on me to help. The first step to luring me in. This is all going according to her plan. You can't trust her."

I looked back at the bed, to the sleeping child. "I can't trust anything that's said inside this room. How do I know *you* aren't trying to trick me?"

Rachel smiled. "Do you sense I'm lying?"

I closed my eyes and blocked out the noise of the ventilators. I focused on the only sound I knew was real.

Plop.
Plop.
Plop.

Somewhere in the distance, that blasted sink was still dripping. As if it was so difficult to get a knob turned. I focused on that sound until it was exploding in my ears. Then I opened my eyes.

The room was as it should be, dark and dilapidated. Rachel was in front of me, eyes rolled up into her head, muscles contracted in her neck, and her body trembling. I looked at the little girl, who was now upright in her bed, eyes pinned on Rachel.

"Let her go!" I yelled at her.

I grabbed Rachel's shoulders and debated how to handle her incarceration. I couldn't fight the beast, since our power was the same, but surely I could give it a push.

Without the coven's link, however, I didn't know where to start. Instead, I just ducked down and bent the woman over my shoulder.

If all else fails, run.

I carried Rachel as fast as I could to the door.

"Hennie!" a graveled voice sounded behind me. The little girl was looking at me. "Remember what I said." She spoke with impossible vocal depth. "I didn't lie."

CHAPTER 37

I STOOD AGAINST THE wall watching the coven piece Rachel back together with their combined power. We had confiscated a room on the lower level, and no one interrupted, since it looked like a prayer circle to the average passerby.

"What happened up there?" Paula asked.

"The usual bullshit," I said. "It's graduated to intelligent provoking instead of the passive stuff, so that's a plus. Pretty soon, I won't be able to tell you two apart."

Paula narrowed her eyes. "What did it say?"

"As I said, bullshit." I pushed away from the wall and headed out. "I'm going home. You can tell me what the plan is tomorrow."

As I walked through the foyer with Dane on my heels, I motioned to the secretary. "Don't you wanna say goodbye to your girl?" I asked.

Dane chuckled. "What's the matter, Hennie? I thought we had an open relationship. You, me, Paul, and Judy."

"Judy?" I pushed through the exit doors and headed to the parking lot. The wind had come up, threatening a storm—possibly even a tornado, if we were lucky. "You two are on a first-name basis already. Please tell me you used a pseudonym."

"Blain."

"Ah, Blain, that's good. Actually, you would make a good Blain."

"You can hardly be jealous of a simple conversation."

"I'm not jealous, dipshit. I'm mad."

"Even after what I saw you and Paula—Paul doing the other day?"

"I can't speak to my mental state when I'm around him, but I am certain you knew exactly what you were doing with that girl, and you made sure I saw it."

"You're damn right I did."

"Why?" I reached the car and turned back to him. "To hurt me? To make me feel like shit? To let me know that at any moment you'll abandon me if I can't live up to your expectations?" My eyes watered and I tried to blink them away, but the tears came out to spite me.

Dane frowned and came to me. I tried to push him away, but he persisted in embracing me. "I'm sorry, Hennie. I shouldn't have done that. I was angry. It's hard seeing you with him."

"It's not the same as another man, you know. He's the freaking devil."

"I know." Dane kissed my temple. "And he only comes out to influence you or incite me. It's just more manipulation. You would think I would be immune to it by now." Dane pulled away and looked at me. "I didn't flirt any longer than it took you to get up the stairs. I told you before, I only want you." He kissed me. For a long moment, we leaned against the car, making out like teenagers.

"I can give you more proof of my devotion back at the house." Dane tugged the car door open behind me and ushered me into the passenger seat. He ran around to the driver's side and hopped in. He started the engine, and we drove off.

After a few minutes of silent driving, he glanced at me. "So, what did happen up there?"

"I had a conversation with Rachel—or rather, I thought it was Rachel. In actuality, it was the beast. It's getting rather good a puppeteering that little girl."

"What do you mean?"

"The voiceover's a little off, but I'm sure in time it will get worked out. Pretty soon she'll be singing creepy lullabies to me."

Dane frowned but continued to stare out at the road ahead of him. "No, I meant what do you mean about the little girl?"

"The little girl that the beast has possessed—or assimilated—whatever." Dane's frown didn't lessen. He continued to glance at me, seeking further explanation. I laughed at his ineptitude. "The little girl that was ripping me to shreds the last time we were there."

Dane stared out at the road, his mouth gaping as he planned his words. "Hennie, there was no little girl. The room was empty."

It was my turn to wear the face of confusion. "Then who ripped me to shreds?"

Dane looked at me, giving me more eye contact than a good driver should. The confounded expression on his face turned to pure shock.

"*You* did."

CHAPTER 38

I SAT ON THE edge of my bed, trying to retrace my steps to see where I had gone wrong. "I don't understand." It wasn't the first time I had said it. It wouldn't be the last.

"I never saw a little girl, Hennie." Dane spoke over a mouthful of toothpaste. He was standing at my door, wet, covered in nothing but a small towel. He was glorious, not that I was taking the time to enjoy it. "I never saw the beast either. No demons. No shadows. The room was empty."

"How is that possible? You see everything I *don't* see. You even see my shadow."

"Yes, but I didn't see anything in that room aside from you having a fit, screaming at thin air, and ripping apart your skin like a fiend."

"But you felt it, right? That oppressive energy?"

"Yes, I felt that, but..."

"But what?"

"I don't know for certain if what I felt was from the beast. You said yourself you didn't feel anything negative in that room. Doesn't its presence normally put you on edge?"

"Yes, but I thought since it was assimilated, it was better at disguising itself. Dane, if you didn't feel the beast, what did you feel?"

"You." He removed the toothbrush from his mouth. "How do you think I find you so easily? You are a beacon to me." He left the doorway, and I listened to him spitting out his toothpaste and putting away his brush. He came back to the door. He watched me, waiting for the question that was waiting in the wings.

"A beacon of evil?" I finally asked.

"No." He pulled his towel off and ran it over his hair once more before tossing it in the hamper next to my dresser. He approached me, putting himself in my face. "I've told you on more than one occasion that I desire to hunt you. I've never wanted to explain that sensation because it doesn't make me look very good, but I'll try since it's better than what you're imagining."

He reached down and tugged my shirt over my head. I raised my arms, allowing the disrobing. "What I said in the hospital was accurate. I felt alive, on the precipice of death, but alive. As if narrowly escaping it."

I thought back to how I'd felt after my brush with death. I could understand the terror-fueled exhilaration.

Dane unclasped my bra and tossed it away. "I generally feel that way when I'm close to you. As if I have narrowly escaped death and I want to make every moment last a lifetime. Every kiss. Every fuck. Even every boring Sunday afternoon."

Dane pushed me back and undid my pants. He took the jeans and the panties underneath with one forceful effort. My shoes were already off, so they were in the hamper a moment later. "Now, when you run. That's a different thing."

Dane yanked off my socks and tickled my feet. I screeched and kicked. When he released my legs, I scooted further up on the bed. He, of course, followed.

"When you run, I feel a primal urge to follow. To find you." He grabbed my legs and spread them apart. He dipped down and kissed my thighs. When he reached my center, he looked up at me. "When you run from me, I become a predator, and you become my prey."

He dove onto me, not allowing me to translate his statement in any way other than carnal. His tongue sent riptides of pleasure down to my toes. Even as delectation overtook my senses, I wondered how it was that I had gone into a room to face the beast and only faced myself.

And more important than that: with three different perceptions about the threat before us, who was lying?

CHAPTER 39

I WAVED AWAY DANE'S intrusive finger. I had never known him to be so playful, especially after sex. He was usually the pass-out-until-morning type of guy. Upon the third nose poke, I grumbled, "Get away, Dane."

A chirping giggle that didn't belong to a man followed. My eyes flapped open. My visions of the childlike beast disappeared when I saw Jess kneeling on the bed beside me.

"Jess! Jesus! You scared the shit out of me." I pushed myself up in bed.

"You are kinda jumpy lately."

"Can you blame me? Please tell me you're here to tell me what the hell is going on."

"Mmm." Jess's lips scrunched up, and she shook her head. "Actually, I'm here for the leftover pizza in your fridge."

I chuckled at her joke. She, meanwhile, scooted off the bed and headed out my bedroom door. I heard her light footsteps trample down the stairs. I glanced over at Dane and considered waking him. I was curious if he would be able to see Jess or if his vision only worked on evil entities.

By the time I got downstairs, Jess had already pulled our latest pizza order from the fridge, along with two sodas and part of a raspberry cheesecake I couldn't finish the first time around.

"Oh, man, I miss food," she exclaimed before taking a bite of the cold pizza.

I laughed at her enthusiasm. "No food in the afterlife?" I asked.

"No body; no food. We survive on the ethereal flow of energy." She spoke as if she were an advertisement for heaven. "Sustaining ourselves with the love and generosity of humanity."

"Sounds nice."

"Oh, don't get me wrong, I love it, but I also love pizza." Jess took another big bite and popped the tab on her soda. She guzzled down some before offering me the second one.

I shook my head. "No, I'm good. I still plan on going back to bed after you leave."

"Suit yourself." She shrugged and continued to moan and groan about the taste and texture of the food.

I wanted desperately to ask her about the beast and everything that was going on in my life, but I also didn't want to interrupt her enjoyment. Who was I to dictate how she haunted me? And besides that, it felt normal. Us, sitting in my mother's gourmet kitchen, chowing down on carb-heavy food.

Despite my so-called delight, a tear dribbled down my cheek. Jess noticed me wiping it away and gave me a sympathetic look. "Bad day?" she asked over a mouthful of cheesecake.

"Yeah, turns out the devil might be playing me for a fool, but I can't figure out where the lie is."

"No one can lie to you, Hennie. Not even the beast."

"Then how can they all be telling me the truth?"

"Truth is in the interpretation. If I believe it to be true, it's the truth. I could say, I'm going to eat this entire box of pizza. I wouldn't be lying because I really do want to, but in reality, I'll be stuffed after two pieces." She took another bite. "See? Perception."

"How do I fight the beast? Or is it even really here?"

"Oh, it's really here. That bastard's seeping into this reality like an infestation. It definitely has to be stopped."

"And *I* have to do it?"

"Yup. You and—" Jess hissed through her teeth. "—dare I say it? The ex."

"That's not funny. You know she kicked me out of the coven."

"Good. You don't need a coven."

"Yeah, who needs access to God's power? Certainly not the devil."

"The devil already has access to God's power. Dane was right, power is power. It's what you do with it that makes it good or bad."

"But if that's true, why do I need Rachel to defeat the beast? My power just bounces right off him and back at me."

Jess bit her lip as if I had just said something monumentally stupid, and she was trying not to tell me so. "Listen." She came around the island and grabbed my hands. "You know I love you, right?"

"Yeah." I almost pulled away from the embrace, since she was being so serious. I couldn't handle more serious.

"You know, if it were up to me, I would tell you the whole spiel and give away the ending, right?"

"But you can't?" I asked somberly.

"I can't!" Jess threw her arms up as if she were yelling at God for her clamped tongue. "They are going on and on about chickens hatching and little baby turtles trekking across the beach." She returned her attention to me, grabbing my shoulders. "You're one of those turtles, Hennie. I want so much to pick you up and walk you to the sea, but I can't because it's the journey that makes you stronger. It's the journey that teaches the lessons you need. And damn it if those fucking seagulls aren't going to give you hell on the way, but I can't pick you up. No matter how much I want to." Jess's hands dropped and her shoulders slumped. She looked at me despairingly.

"It's okay, Jess." I patted her arms. "I understand."

"The thing is..." Jess moved back to her pizza, but instead of eating, she paced the length of the island. "I don't think you need to be picked up so much as nudged. Maybe you haven't looked at this from the right perspective. Maybe you need to look at it from someone else's perspective. Someone unbiased to your outcome. Someone who cares for you, but also kind of hates you."

"Rachel?"

"Yeah, maybe she has some insight into this overlapping possession-slash-beast situation."

"Great. Yet another marked moment of awkwardness to look forward to. Maybe we'll make up and become the best of friends."

Jess frowned. "I thought *I* was your best friend."

I laughed. "You are." My smile died as I looked at her. "You were."

"Uck, don't remind me." Jess dove back into her pizza, as if remembering she had a limited amount of time to enjoy it.

Chapter 40

"YOU SHOULDN'T BE HERE," Rachel said when she opened the door to her classroom. The new convent was still being renovated to accommodate their needs, but the sisters still had Sunday school classes, group counseling sessions, and parenting classes to head up. I'd found out the community center was sponsoring Bible school for the summer, and I assumed Rachel would be the one teaching it. She was, after all, one of the few real nuns in the coven. For many of them, the path of the sisterhood was more about the witchcraft than the prayers, though I had found some solace in both.

"I need to talk to you."

"Tell Paula I am still praying on the matter."

I put my foot in the door before she could close it. "I'm not here about that." She paused, waiting to hear me out, if only for a moment. "I'm here for..." I rolled my eyes, because I knew how stupid it sounded. "...guidance."

Rachel stared at me, no emotion on her face beyond her discontent at the disruption. Her foot kicked hard into mine, pushing it clear of the door. Then she shut it in my face.

I stared through the glass as she went back to her students, apologizing for the interruption. An icy coolness spread over me, not dissimilar to what I had felt inside of the circle after the coven had broken from me.

I was understanding it better. A craving for revenge, spawning from pain, rejection, and sorrow. I knew these emotions very well. I wondered if they were worse than anger. I already knew what my power could do when I was mad. What could they do when I was sad?

Instead of reaching for the power, I took a calming breath and pushed it away. Regardless of how hurt I was, I wouldn't take it out on Rachel. Maybe I was clinging too tightly to the angelic moment we'd shared in the basement. I was expecting too much from her. After all, she was still Rachel.

She was as stubborn and stone-hearted as I was. More so in some ways. At least she could put on a smile and dress up like a clown or teach Sunday school kids. What had *I* ever done to make the world a better place? Granted, dispatching bad people made the world suck less, but it didn't make it better.

I turned away from the door and headed down the hall in search of the vending machines I had passed. I thought my efforts at civility merited a chocolate reward.

"After class," Rachel hollered down the hall after me. I turned back and saw her hanging out her door. I opened my mouth to thank her, but she tucked back inside and slammed the door.

Hell *yes*, I deserved chocolate.

CHAPTER 41

I'M ASHAMED TO ADMIT I used my magic to get several free candy bars from the vending machines. When Rachel finally tracked me down following a trail of teenagers, she found me cross-legged on the floor, covered in wrappers and smudged with chocolate.

I looked up at her and took a bite out of the Snickers that was getting melty between my fingers. "Don't judge me," I mumbled over my mouthful. "Want some?" I kicked the machine closest to my feet and made a bag of M&M's eject from the confines of the coils trapping it.

Rachel looked down at the candy through the window. To my surprise, she reached in and pulled it out. She ripped the top off and pulled one of the coated candies out to admire it before popping it in her mouth. She found a nearby folding chair and pulled it over closer to me and sat down. For a moment, we both sat there and ate candy. It was nice to ignore the animosity that had been building between us.

"I didn't get a chance to see if you were all right after the hospital," I began. "I assume there was no lasting damage."

"A bit of a kick to my ego. That's all."

"Yeah, the beast tends to do that."

"Is that what you came here for? To check on me?"

I snorted. "I wish. That would make me sound thoughtful." I licked some chocolate off my fingers before it ended up on my face. "I'm afraid my motives are entirely selfish."

"Motives usually are."

"It's just... I'm not as schooled in the Bible as you. Sister Aggie helped me understand what was happening to me when this all started. If things had turned out differently, I would be going to Paula instead. But they didn't. So, I'm left with questions I can't answer. And you are the only one that can. I just wasn't sure if you would."

"I'm listening."

Rather than piss around, I got straight to the point. "When you were taken over by the beast, it spoke to me—through you. At first I thought you were lecturing me, but then I realized you were warning me. You said Paula was tricking us to get into that room together—to unite our powers. And then afterward, when we failed, Paula would take advantage of the situation to get control of me—or something to that effect."

"And you believed this?"

"That's the problem. I can sense a lie, even on Paula. She's very careful not to lie to me. She'll circle the truth sometimes, but an outright lie I can tell. She wasn't lying about the situation in that room. But the beast also wasn't lying about her plotting against me."

"Perhaps neither one of them is lying. Maybe Paula does want to remove the beast, but she also wants to take advantage of you."

"If that's true, then I'm walking into a trap and there is nothing I can do to change it. The beast can't be assimilated, so I have to help stop it."

"Which means you will have to face Paula after you are done with the beast."

I shook my head. "I don't think she's going to fight me. That won't turn out well. The beast said Paula would use *you* against me."

"How?"

"I'm not sure, but I can only assume she'll threaten you in some way. It's quite possible we're both walking into a trap."

"Are you saying I shouldn't help you?"

I shrugged. "That's why I'm here. Obviously I'm dangerous, and so is Paula, but the beast has no compass or direction. It's pure rage. If Paula is telling the truth, then we both *have* to be there, regardless of what happens after."

"What is it you fear from Paula?" Rachel asked, sounding the part of a psychiatrist.

I looked up and shook my head at her. "I know you think I'm an abomination, but I'm not ready to die. I'm not ready to return to the trinity."

"I see. And what, if anything, would change your mind? What would she have to do to convince you to merge voluntarily?"

I looked away. "Threaten the people I love."

Rachel said nothing for a long moment. I could tell she was trying to sidestep the gigantic pile of awkwardness I had dropped on her.

"Sometimes there's only one path to choose," Rachel finally said. "It may be a rocky path, but eventually it will lead to a fork. Then you choose which direction you want to go."

I scoffed. "That's it? That's all you got? Fortune cookie logic?"

Rachel sighed and stood up. "What can I say? This entire situation is shit. I don't want to go into that room any more than you do, but we obviously have to. It's the only way to set things right." Rachel turned to walk away.

"What does the Big Man say about it?"

Rachel froze. "What do you mean?"

"I mean, you've prayed on it, right? Any signs or hints as to the right course of action?"

"No," she said. I could sense the lie, as I always did. "It doesn't matter, though. God has nothing to do with the affairs of the devil. We're on our own with this one."

"Wait. One more thing." Rachel stopped again and looked back at me, perturbed. I was pushing my luck now. "What did you see inside that room?"

Rachel frowned. "What do you mean?"

"When I went in there, I saw a little girl, but Dane said he didn't see her. What did you see?"

"I..." She shook her head. "It didn't appear that way for me."

"How did it appear to you?"

Rachel shifted and looked out the far windows facing the parking lot. "It appeared as me. I had a good long argument with myself about morality. Next thing I knew, I was waking up with my coven around me. I'm afraid I don't even remember you showing up. Why? Does it matter that we all saw different things?"

I shrugged. "I suppose not. The beast is whatever it wants to be."

"Rest up, Hennie. I'll see you later." Rachel glided away, freeing herself from further conversation. I wondered why she had lied about God's weigh-in on this fight. Did he not want us to go after the beast? Was it too dangerous? Or was he protecting the devil as he had before? Regardless of the reason, I didn't like that Rachel was keeping it to herself.

CHAPTER 42

I SAT IN THE back of the bowling alley, listening to the balls roll, the pins drop, and the machinery putting them back again. From this angle, the task was disturbingly futile. Although, I wasn't sure where the hopelessness lay. Was it the endless cycle of trying to put back together what the balls had broken? Or did the frustration revolve around the fact that even after the balls had collapsed the pins, they would just rise back up, again and again, without fail?

"Are you ready?" Paula asked beside me.

I slowly shifted myself in the folding chair to face her. "How much longer do we have to do this?"

"Don't you want to help people?" she asked.

"I'm not helping anyone. The people you bring to me are in pain or angry. The requests are unnecessary or irrational. At what point do people just have to live their life, burdened by the mundane or the morose?"

"I think you'll like this one," she said with a glimmer of amusement in her eye. "Sit back. And listen closely. You won't want to miss anything."

I sat back in the chair and waited. A young woman appeared out of nowhere on the other side of the card table. As usual, she seemed to understand instantly why she was there. There was never any surprise or shock at having suddenly arrived in the back of a bowling alley, staring at a nun and her punkish sidekick.

"What do you want?" I asked flatly.

"I want to die," she said.

My tired eyes widened into alertness. I hadn't expected something so simple. My thoughts were immediately sympathetic to the woman. As someone familiar with the type of pain that begged for a cessation of life, I knew it could be a heavy burden.

As my immediate pity wavered, my logical thought processes took over. Suicide, though frequently shamed, was an easy enough task to accomplish on one's own. It certainly didn't require the help of the devil.

"If you desire to die, why haven't you taken your own life?" I asked gingerly.

The woman shook her head and looked down at her lap. "I can't." She lifted her hands from her lap and set them on top of the card table.

Wrapped around her wrists was a tight wire. The thin metal overlapped itself at least a dozen times. Each ring cut deep into the woman's flesh. The oldest cuts had scabbed over. I could even see one area where a scab had grown over the wire, causing the skin to buckle and ooze if she shifted just right.

I took a breath that sufficed as a quiet gasp. I already knew the answer to my question before she spoke.

"I am being held captive." She sounded almost ashamed to admit it, as if her situation embarrassed her.

"Shouldn't you be requesting your freedom? Or better yet, wouldn't you like your captor to be caught and punished for his crimes? Or perhaps I could kill him for you?" I wasn't sure why I was offering to murder her captor. I knew what it made me sound like, but it was a good way to gauge this woman's true motives.

The woman looked surprised that I would suggest homicide over suicide. She glanced at Paula, but shook her head. "I don't wish to sully my soul with revenge. I only wish to alleviate my own distress."

"Why should you die, though? Certainly, we could find you a way to escape."

"I have been imprisoned too long. I have no energy left to survive. I know God is watching me. I know my trials are necessary, but I am tired. If he will not guide me home, then I will seek guidance elsewhere. I have invited the devil inside of me. I don't care what games he plays or what promises he breaks. I only ask that when he is through, I be allowed to die. To rise to heaven, as I am intended."

"Wait a minute." I looked at Paula and found her simpering at me. "She's already opened herself to you?"

"Indeed. She's one of mine now."

I threw my hands up and slammed them down on the card table. The woman across from me jumped and pulled her hands away. "This is insane. You could starve yourself. You could find a way to puncture a vein. You don't go ass first onto a platter and ask to get screwed just so you can get permission to die."

"Does that mean you'll do it?" Paula asked.

"Do what?" I asked.

"Will you kill her?"

"Kill her?" I drew myself back from Paula, trying to get a better view of the crazy on her. "Why do I have to kill her?"

"This woman has been taken captive. She has suffered abuses at the hands of her captor. Out of desperation, she invited in another enemy. In return for her offering, she is requesting to die when we are through with her. The question is quite simple. Will we allow that to happen or not?"

"What happens if I don't say yes?"

The woman across from me let out a loathsome bark, unable to control her tears. She curled into a ball and rocked on her chair.

"You mean besides making this poor woman go through potentially years of torture?" Paula asked sarcastically.

"Yes, besides that," I snapped.

"She will remain possessed by choice and captive against her will. She will be unable to control any aspect of her life. She will not be able to commit suicide without our help."

"I can't believe you're leaving this up to me. You're the one possessing her, you decide."

"I'm afraid I can't decide this on my own. This is one of those moral choices that requires a conscience. After all, if I had my way, I would bleed the little bitch out until there was barely anything human left inside of her."

I narrowed my eyes at her. There was a slight lie in what she was saying. Not an outright lie, but more of an exaggeration. That fine line between saying you hate someone, when really you just don't like them at the moment. I suspected the statement would be more true out of the lips of the serpent or the beast. Despite all four of us being part of one another, the separation had taken its toll. Life as a human had softened Paula.

Though being the soul of the devil had already put me one step ahead in the morality column. There was no doubt in my mind that living as a human, being raised by loving parents, had fostered my compassion for mankind, in a way that hanging out in hell never could have.

Had Paula come into this world as a child with loving parents and supportive friends, perhaps she too would have a little more than a lingering affection for humans.

"What about the games she's talking about? How long are you going to make those last? I see no point in granting her death if you're going to keep her going for months and months, anyway. If I'm going to grant a humane death, then I at least need to know she won't be half-dead before it arrives."

Paula shrugged. "I'm almost done playing with her. She's not the most enthusiastic possession I've ever done, but there's no sense wasting a perfectly susceptible vessel."

I looked at the woman and she looked back at me, eyes wide and eager to hear my answer. I took another moment to think about what I was doing. It was a slippery slope, deciding the fate of your fellow man. But as I saw it, this was nothing more than a physician-assisted suicide. In this case, a systematically assisted suicide. As much as I didn't want to be responsible for the death of another human being, I also didn't want to be responsible for the suffering of one. No one had consulted me before taking possession of this poor woman, so I only had the choice of life or death. Given that she was already in a horrific situation physically and mentally before my ilk had arrived, I decided the only humane decision was to ease her pain and reduce her suffering.

I looked at Paula, expecting to see a wide smirk on her face, but there was no humor in her expression. She was looking at me curiously, possibly evaluating if I was ready to turn back to the dark side. As I saw it, there was no light side in this scenario.

I turned to the woman across the table. She took a breath and held it as I opened my mouth to speak. "I will grant you death when the devil is done with you."

CHAPTER 43

I FELT DIRTY AND vindicated at the same time. It was as if my skin was crawling, trying to get the feeling of the icky tendrils of evil off me. I even felt a little sick, like I had taken a full dose of magic and was paying for the hangover. And yet I had done nothing. I had used no power. Only the power of choice.

I knew I had made the right decision. I knew alleviating pain was more important than my respect for life. However, being the one metaphorically holding the knife made it feel far more unseemly.

Fearful that I had just fallen down a rabbit hole and was heading straight to hell, I drove home as fast as I could. I locked myself inside of my house and said a few quick prayers, hoping to wash away my guilt. When it didn't help, I searched the house for a cross or rosary. I eventually remembered my necklace, the one with the little silver cross I used to wear under my robe at the convent.

I rushed up to my room and found it hanging where I had left it. The retired cross dangled from the twist switch on my vanity lamp. I looped my fingers into the chain and lifted it. I whispered another prayer, which wasn't much more than a bunch of pleases in a row. I pinched my fingers around the little cross and held it tight. I clenched my teeth waiting for the sound of the sizzle and the smell of burning skin. I waited nearly a minute, as if it were a pregnancy test that required a little time to reveal the truth. I lifted my thumb and checked it for burns. Aside from the discolored skin where I had pressed an impression of the cross into it, there was nothing.

I wasn't evil.

I hadn't backslid with my decision.

I may have been morally objectionable, but I had not dragged my feet through the pit of hell.

Not yet, anyway.

CHAPTER 44

I SHUDDERED AS I stepped through the doors to the hospital. Once again, there was nothing different about its physical space. And yet, the shadows were bending the wrong way. The air felt hot and cold at the same time. Every footstep echoed through the space a little longer than a natural reverberation should.

Something had changed.

The beast was stronger.

Or perhaps I was just more afraid.

Whatever was about to happen would no doubt be tiresome, painful, and emotionally shattering, but what else could I do? I couldn't allow the beast to walk the Earth. It was bad enough Paula flaunted her human form as a member of a religious order. The last thing we needed was a ten-year-old gathering minions for a new hell on earth via the local playground.

"Are you okay?" Dane rested his hand on my shoulder.

"Sure, why would I be scared? I'm only about to face the most powerful being on Earth."

"I know, but you're scratching the hell out of your arm." He motioned to my bicep.

I looked down at my left hand digging into my right arm like it was a clawing post. There were streaks of raw red skin and in several spots, a little blood was even peeking through. I forced my hand down and shook my head as if the act was a nervous tick, when in reality I hadn't even been aware I was doing it. Apparently, I was dreading this fight even more than I realized.

"Come on, you two." Paula pushed past us. "Time to get this show on the road."

I followed Paula up the stairs with Dane at my back. I noticed the faces of the people we passed. Their eyes lingered on us, as if we were an aberration of nature. They all seemed to sense something I didn't.

The closer we got to our destination, the darker it got. Though I was positive the sun was still shining brightly outside, the only proof of it was the dusty glowing rays that came to an abrupt stop not long after they pierced through the curtains in the rooms.

I glanced back at Dane to see if he was feeling the same thing I was. He was watching the patients and nurses that passed us. His watchful gaze turned more virulent with each passing face.

I felt a grip on my wrist and assumed Paula was ushering me along, but when I turned back, I saw a nurse dressed in a pristine white uniform—not of this decade. "I look forward to watching the beast eat you alive," she said, eyes glimmering with delight.

"Get off her!" Dane grabbed the woman and threw her into the wall. When she hit the wall, her uniform instantly transformed into pale green scrubs. The woman looked fearfully at Dane before scurrying off in tears.

"Ignore them," Paula said. She had stopped to wait for us to catch up. "This place is flooded with demons. They're piggybacking for the fun of it. No sense in entertaining them more than we already will be in a moment."

Dane moved up beside me, ushering me closer to the wall. I was certain his intention was to corral me away from the passersby, but that still left the patients in the rooms we passed to heckle me.

"You'll never defeat him," an old man rasped from his bed in one of the rooms.

An old woman with a walker tried to grab me on the way by. "To the fiery pits of hell with you! Traitor!" She spat at me before I could get clear. I wiped away the assault, not wanting to retaliate against an innocent vessel.

Dane pulled me closer, and we both ignored the rest of the taunts, which became increasingly more lewd and disturbing.

By the time we reached the room, Dane had shifted me forward again so he could watch me. From my perspective, the halls were empty, but I knew from his watchful gaze that there were still plenty of demons here to be leery of. Just because there were no puppets for them didn't mean I was safe.

"How many?" I asked.

"Too many," he answered.

"It's a full house tonight," Paula—who at some point had transformed into Paul—said as he reached the double doors leading into the room. He stopped and looked back at me. He reached out for my hand as if he were asking me to dance. I stared at the outstretched hand for a moment. "Come now, Hennie, they're all waiting."

I placed my palm against his, and I felt a ripple of power from him. He winked at me before leading me inside to begin the battle.

CHAPTER 45

THE CIRCLE OF WOMEN sitting cross-legged on the floor was a welcome sight. Their steady chanting warmed the otherwise cool room. There was even a glow emanating from them like candlelight. They were all so beautiful: faces, hearts, souls. I hated that I could no longer feel them. Their minds, even as unconscious as the bond had been, had felt like family. Now my only family was Dane.

I looked back to see why he hadn't joined us yet. I saw through the tall slender window in the door that he was holding a 2x4. He slipped it along the outside of the door, presumably through the handles. He was locking us in.

He looked up at me through the window. He pressed his hand against the glass and mouthed the words, "I love you."

I simply nodded to him and he turned around, cracking his knuckles and looking over the *full house* Paul had earlier referred to.

"Dane will keep the riff-raff away," Paul assured me. "It's best he stays out of the way of our immediate interactions, anyway. Last thing we need is a hostage situation." Paul smirked at me. I frowned at the humor he found in that statement. As far as I was concerned, we were already in the middle of a negotiation for a hostage, but it was probably best that Dane wasn't the victim. I was far less attached to the little girl in this room than I was to him.

I looked to the far end of the room, beyond the coven. I could see her. She was out of her bed, standing at the foot of it. Her eyes locked onto me, staring me down like a starving wolf.

I wondered why she didn't attack. Get to me while I was still figuring out my next move. I wanted to blame it on the coven—they could have been putting up a protection spell—but I knew that wasn't it. She was waiting.

The beast was waiting.

Rachel removed herself from the circle and joined me and Paul—who was now back in his female form.

"Will you stop changing forms?" I complained to her. "I can barely keep track of you as it is."

Paula chuckled and turned to Rachel. "Are you ready?"

"I guess. Are you sure this is the right way to do this?" Rachel glanced back at the beast. I wondered what she saw this time. Was it still herself? Was she battling her own demons—literally?

Paula narrowed her eyes. "If you can think of a better way to solve this situation, then I am all ears. Quite frankly, you are the only one with any usable power here. We're just your backup, so unless *you* are ready, Hennie and I can go get a coffee."

Rachel frowned and looked at me. "Has she explained how difficult this is going to be?"

I glanced at Paula, who crossed her arms rather than answer. "I've fought the beast before. I know my power is useless against it."

"Yes, but I will be able to hurt it. That, in turn, may hurt you. You will have to fight through it."

I hadn't thought about that. I knew anything that hurt my shadow hurt me, but I'd assumed the beast would be exempt from that connection, like Paula was. "I'll do what I need to," I stated bravely, even though I caught myself clawing at my arm again. Rachel noticed it, but I pretended not to be disturbed by my uncontrollable manic behavior.

"Okay then, let's step inside the circle." Rachel entered through the broken hands, followed by me and Paula. The moment we passed the boundary, I felt safe, embraced by a familiar power—one I hadn't experienced since Sister Aggie's possession.

It shouldn't have made any difference. Power was power. But there was definitely something appealing about the light end of the spectrum versus the dark end. Maybe it had something to do with purity or strength, but it felt as much like home to me as hell's addictive embrace. I presumed that was because I belonged to both worlds. The soul of the devil was sanctified, after all. Born in the heavens, banished to hell—a world of our own creation. The devil may not have wanted to return to the pearly gates, but there was likely a part of him that still craved it.

I looked around at the faces of my former coven. Meredith opened her eyes as I looked at her. She gave me a slight nod before returning to her concentrated spell work. The others didn't raise their gazes to me, but I knew they could sense me. In this confined space, the power ebbing off me was no doubt just as appealing to them as theirs was to me.

"Take my hand, Hennie," Paula said and gripped my hand in hers. Rachel took my other hand, and I stood between them, sandwiched between good and evil. "Do you feel it?" Paula asked as she sucked in a breath between her teeth. "I always was envious of his power. I was never quite as strong as he was. But I suppose that was intentional."

"The coven will protect us, but we need to stay inside the circle. Do you understand?" Rachel looked at me and I nodded. I had no intention of leaving the circle. If I had it my way, I would walk about throughout my day with the sisters at my back. Then again, I was a magic junkie, so that was no surprise.

As it was, it was difficult to keep my own connection to hell subdued. I could feel Paula tempting me. The tiny shimmer of energy that coursed through our connection was slightly arousing in more ways than one. Rachel's energy was not as stimulating, but rather relaxing. Between the two, I felt exhilarated but calm.

I reminded myself that I was only here to support Rachel. To protect her and heal her as needed from the beast's retaliation.

"Shall we begin?" Paula asked.

Rachel nodded and closed her eyes. She took in a deep breath. When she opened them again, they looked slightly fogged. Paula did something similar, but her eyes turned black. I took the cue and inhaled in my last easy breath. I closed my eyes, but when I opened them, a blooming fire had risen between the coven and the little girl on the other side.

The battle had begun.

CHAPTER 46

A RIPTIDE OF ENERGY flooded my veins. My own? Rachel's? Paula's? I didn't know. All I knew was the fire lashing my face and the pain in my gut.

I screamed and pushed power into Rachel. She took a breath, feeling the overwhelming rush. She barely afforded me a glance before throwing more of her magic at the firewall before us.

The chanting around me drowned out the roar and crackle of the dying fire. I looked at the little girl. She was writhing in pain. The exorcism was working.

I chanted with the other witches and kneeled down to rest my aching body. Paula glanced at me, annoyed perhaps by my prayers.

Rachel yelled the words above me even as she propelled an onslaught of white fire at the beast. I felt each impact like a punch, but I breathed through the pain. The more it hurt me, the more I put into Rachel. The more I put into her, the more Paula put into me. It was a magical chain I wasn't sure I belonged in, but it was working.

As the pain worsened, I wondered why I couldn't be at home eating pizza and watching an 80s movie instead of fighting this war. Paula could have protected Rachel and fed her strength. My power was coming from her, anyway.

I looked at the little girl across the room. She was getting weak. Crumpled on the floor, she watched us with a look of misery on her face. The beast wasn't fighting nearly as hard as I'd thought he would. If anything, the battle was going much too easily. For Rachel, at least. *I* was feeling pummeled.

I looked at Paula, but she didn't seem nearly as affected by the trauma. I wasn't sure whether she was tougher than me or whether she was simply immune to the abuses the rest of us shared. Or maybe she was saving some of her magic to block herself from the pain.

Possibly all the above.

I looked back at the little girl, and she looked at me. For the first time, I noticed something I hadn't seen the first time I looked at her. Granted, I had seen her from a distance—and she had been kicking my ass at the time—but I was still surprised I hadn't recognized her.

Rachel had said that she'd seen herself in this room. I'd thought it was a strange incarnation until now.

This wasn't just some random little girl staring back at me. It was me.

Me at ten years old, but still me.

I felt another hit, and I dropped to the floor. I nearly passed out, or perhaps I did pass out, because when I looked back up, everyone was gone.

CHAPTER 47

"You know you can't win." Sister Aggie sat on an iron bedframe under one of the windows. She was sitting casually, leaning back, smoking a cigarette.

"You're not real," I said to her as I glanced around the vacant room for the coven or even the beast—someone to prove that I was still in the right place.

"Aren't I?" she asked. "I'm probably more real than you are." She stood up and crushed her cigarette out under her boot heel. Naturally, she was wearing her robe and habit. I had rarely seen her in any other clothes, so I didn't imagine my mind could hallucinate her any other way.

"You are just an idea," Aggie said as she sauntered toward me. "A fragment."

"I'm a soul."

"Yes, someone else's soul."

"Which one are you? Are you the beast? Are you the serpent?"

"Who said I'm any of them? Maybe I really am Sister Aggie."

"And why would she come here? Why now? I'm about to perform an exorcism. She wouldn't want to interfere with that."

"She would if she knew you were making a grave mistake."

"And what mistake is that?"

"The same mistake I made by bringing you onboard with us. I should have let you kill yourself. We all would have been better off."

I pushed down the emotions that were loosed by her words. I knew this wasn't Sister Aggie. I knew she would never say that to me. This had to be the beast. It was distracting me—trying to get me to retaliate. I wouldn't. Not while everyone was in danger around me. I was not the serpent, or the ram, or the beast—I was Hennie, and I was in control of my emotions.

"Fuck you!"

Most of them.

Aggie laughed. "There she is. That stubborn teenage girl who beats up the girls that make fun of her."

"What do you want?"

"I want you to once and for all realize that you can't get away from who you are."

"I'm not going back. I'm not going to rejoin the trinity."

"You will eventually. Why put everyone at risk to do this? Why not simply accept your responsibility? I think we both know why you can't."

"And why is that?"

"Because you're selfish."

"Selfish? That's rich coming from the mouth of the devil."

"I'm not the devil."

I frowned. Her words rang true.

"I am Sister Aggie."

My brow deepened, and I shook my head.

"No, it can't be you. You're dead."

"I'm not the first dead person to visit you. We've been trying to help you, but it seems you don't understand what it is you need to do."

"And what is that?"

"Embrace your dark side."

"I did, and it nearly killed me."

"No, you embraced *his* dark side. I'm talking about yours. Find the power within yourself."

"I can't do that again. It's too much. It will destroy me."

Aggie shrugged. "Your path has already been set from the moment you were brought into existence. You can't fight it. You must become what I feared you would become all along. Had I known that I had no chance of preventing it, I wouldn't have made such an effort. You were a waste of my time."

Once again, the words brought out more emotions than I expected. The fact that I could no longer rationalize that these were the words of the devil made it harder to fight the pain.

"Open your eyes, Hennie. See yourself for who you really are."

CHAPTER 48

T HE LITTLE GIRL BEFORE me—myself—reached out her hand and I couldn't help but reach for her as well. However, with my hand clasped to Paula's, I couldn't get very far.

"Help me!" she cried out to me. "Let me go," she whimpered, though I could hear it as clear as day.

"Why are you doing this?" I asked the beast inside of her.

"It's the only way," she answered.

"What's the only way?"

"I can't get out. I can't get away." I realized these were her words, not those of the beast.

"We're trying to get it out of you, I promise," I assured her.

"I'm dying."

"No, hang on, I won't let you die."

"But I must," she insisted. "It's the only way."

"What?"

"I have to be free."

I narrowed my eyes, trying to focus on her. "I don't understand."

"Kill me!" she screamed at me.

I shook my head. "I won't kill you."

"But you promised!"

"I promised what?"

"You promised to kill me when the devil was done playing his games."

My struggle to understand collided with my memories of the woman in the bowling alley. "You were the one I granted the favor to?"

The girl nodded. "You promised to free me from my prison."

"Your prison? You mean remove the beast?"

"No, not him."

The world around me slowed—and not just metaphorically. The air felt stale. The voices of the coven were gone, even though they were all still around me. I wasn't sure whether I was hallucinating or whether I was doing this somehow.

"I invited the devil in," the little girl continued. "I wanted him to help me."

"Help you with what?" I asked, because the thought I was grappling with was too difficult and painful to comprehend.

"I wanted him to help me get rid of you!" the little girl screamed at me with more rage than I'd thought an adolescent capable of. Or perhaps it was the kind of anger only an adolescent could experience.

I frowned at the accusation of my trespassing. "Who are you?" I asked, forcing myself to hear the truth I didn't want to know. The truth I had buried deep, deep inside of myself. Even deeper than my true identity.

"I am Hennie James!" she said somewhat proudly. "The real Hennie. You stole my body," she seethed. "You stole my life."

This was the girl in the coma. Not me, not the person I woke up as in that hospital so many years ago. This was the girl who had slipped into a coma after a car accident. This was the soul I had shoved aside to make room for mine. The human I had been puppeteering for the last decade and a half. The human *I* was possessing.

"I didn't mean to." The words came out as a whisper—littered with guilt. "I just wanted to escape. I wanted—"

"To be free!" she screamed at me. We were so far away, but I could hear her as if she were right in front of me. "So do I. I've been trapped in here with you the whole time. I can't live! I can't die! I'm just stuck."

"What do you want? What can I do?"

"I want to die."

"How?" I asked, willing to do whatever magical ceremony was necessary to appease her soul.

"You must die, so I can die."

Her desperation pained me, but my sympathy quickly evaporated. I shook my head. "No, I can't. I'm not ready to go back."

"You don't belong here."

"Please, let me stay."

"I didn't invite you."

"I know, but God said... I was given permission to stay."

The little girl narrowed her eyes on me and leaned forward as if she were getting in my face over the long distance between us. "Not... by... me." She bolstered up her chest and, with a roar that belonged to a lion instead of a child, she screamed, "GET OUT!"

CHAPTER 49

HOLY WATER SPLASHED ON my face, waking me from an unconscious state, or just reviving my perception. Despite my efforts to maintain my sobriety from evil, the water still stung my eyes. I blinked away blurry vision and tried to orient myself.

My arms were still up, being held in place, but Paula and Rachel were in front of me. They were both reading from Bibles. Though it wouldn't have been an odd vision at the time of meeting Paula, I thought it was extremely out of place now.

"What's happening?" I looked around at the coven. They were all still chanting, hands locked. I remained in the circle, but instead of being leashed by the linked hands of my former sisters, I was shackled. I followed the path of the chains stemming from my handcuffs. The metal links reached all the way up into the rafters, attached to something beyond the torn ceiling tiles. "What's going on?" I rattled the chains, watching them waggle all the way up.

"The spell has worn off," Paula said to Rachel, who gave me a wary look.

"What are you doing?"

"What we came here to do," Rachel said. "We are exorcising a demon."

"I'm not a demon!"

"She knows what you are, Hennie. She understands, as you don't, that you need to leave this Earth. You are much too dangerous to yourself and others." Paula paced around me. "I asked her to help me and she readily agreed."

I looked at Rachel, but she averted her eyes to her Bible and started praying again. "How did you do this?" I asked, surprised that they had manipulated me to the point of hallucination. "The beast. I fought him. I nearly died."

"Yes, you were fighting yourself. Nearly got you killed too, but not quite close enough." Paula held up her pinched fingers. "So I had to concoct another plan. One you couldn't resist." Paula leaned on Rachel's shoulders. She seethed at the contact, but continued to read.

"How?"

"Hennie." Paula answered. "The real Hennie. We had a good long talk with her. She agreed to invite the devil in. In exchange, of course, for your exile so that her body could die and she could ascend to heaven to be with her family."

"She did this?" I asked, trying to comprehend the ultimate betrayal. My own body was plotting against me.

"Isn't it just poetic?" Paula crooned. "I thought you were going to kill yourself with your own magic, but that turned out to be a bust. You bounced right back after you got off the juice. Then this opportunity arose and I couldn't pass it up. Now that the beast has been invited into your body, we can push and pull from all directions. As soon as we exorcize the intruder—aka you—we'll be back to normal. Just the *three* of us."

I looked around at the women who had colluded against me. My eyes landed back on Rachel. "Why? Why would you participate in this?"

She looked up from her book and shook her head. "I'm sorry, Hennie. I really am, but... you were getting too strong. And you will only get stronger."

"I wasn't using the magic anymore! I stopped!"

"I can't trust that you will resist forever. The temptation is too great. You're a threat to all of us. You have to be stopped."

I turned my attention to Paula. I wanted to point out that Rachel was literally joining forces with the devil to accomplish this *good* deed. She was the real threat, but, of course, she was too strong to be banished. Rachel was simply using the enemy-of-my-enemy defense. Not to mention I was certain Paula had put visions of carnage in Rachel's head, painting me as the monster.

Still...

Couldn't she see past it all? Why couldn't she see me for me? I was a good person. I had been balancing two worlds on my shoulders all alone... because she'd left me.

They had all left me.

I felt my disappointment and bitterness over my loneliness cool my core. My anger filtered through betrayal and hurt. Blinded by rejection, I felt raw power bubble up inside of me.

The raw power of a soul.

My soul.

CHAPTER 50

POWER SHOULD HAVE BEEN power. Light, dark, purple, blue, green... What did it matter?

The heavens rained down purity, the fires of hell licked with anger, but I held something else.

Born in heaven and stoked by hell, I had the power of Satan himself.

It wasn't quite right to say that I was Satan. And yet, I was his soul. I was the seed of God's first and most powerful creation.

As I opened the floodgates and embraced the power, it ran through me like a river, healing me, focusing me, and strengthening me. I knew at that moment, without a doubt, I was far stronger than I had ever thought.

I wondered if the reason the serpent had flooded me with so much of his own power was to mask the true power I held inside of me. He filtered the magic he fed me through hellfire. It was powerful, no doubt, but it was nothing compared to the vigor gifted by divinity.

And yet, I wasn't an angel.

I wasn't a demon either.

I was something different.

I was what severed Satan's connection to God. I was what created the fires of hell.

"No," Paula whispered and rambled the text in her Bible.

I saw Rachel's eyes widen as she steadily fell away from me. I realized then that I was rising. With no wings to speak of, it was purely a defiance of physics. There were more gasps around me, and the coven lost track of their chant.

I reached for the cuff on my left wrist and it fell away, disintegrated by my mere touch. I did the same to the right.

"You cannot do this!" Paul said below me—no doubt now in the masculine form in the hopes of controlling me better. With a flick of my finger, I shoved him across the room.

Zero points for male dominance.

I waved my hands and swept the girls away. They slammed into walls, bedframes, and random equipment, guaranteeing that they were knocked out cold.

I descended back down to the ground to face Rachel. She lowered her book and stared at me. She looked worried, but not frightened. "I did this to protect you."

"Bullshit," I said. "You did it for the same reason you kicked me out of the coven. You were jealous. I could have helped you. Together we could have helped so many people. I could have fought by your side. Now we have to fight."

"We don't have to fight, Hennie. This doesn't have to end this way."

"You're right, it doesn't. I can walk away and you can leave me the hell alone."

Rachel's face fell. "You know I can't do that. What you're becoming is unnatural."

"No more unnatural than Paula."

"Paula has limitations. She is bound by rules. You... You're different. You were never supposed to exist. Those rules don't apply to you."

"Because I have a soul. I have the right to choose." I started to walk away, but Rachel rested her hand on me. She barely touched me, but the trembling in her hand was what made me stop.

"Yes." She swallowed hard. "By definition, you have free will. However, you also have a lot of power. Don't you see how compromising that is to your morality? Can't you think clearly enough to see that you will be corrupted by it? Humans are not meant to walk the Earth as gods, Hennie. You must choose to surrender yourself. You must make the hero's choice and sacrifice yourself for the greater good."

I turned and pushed her hand off me. "I'm not the villain or the hero in this. I'm an innocent bystander. So just leave me the fuck alone and I won't have to hurt you."

Rachel's eyes watered, and she shook her head. "I can't. It's my job to fight evil."

"I'm not evil!"

"You will be! Please, Hennie, make this decision while you still have the strength of character to do it without force."

"I'm allowed to be here. God has given me permission to be here. You said so yourself."

Rachel took a breath and shrugged. "I don't remember that conversation—if it even happened at all."

"You still don't believe me?"

"I believe that you believe. I think in a world of demons and magic, we can't always trust what we see."

"I know what I saw. I know what you said. I believed you cared about me then, but I don't believe it now. This is the kindest you have been to me since the day I left, and it's completely fake. I scare the shit out of you. You resent me too. I can feel it. Whatever friendship we had is over. You and I are now enemies. If you come after me..." I let the sentence end there. I didn't know what I would do if she came after me. I didn't want to kill her, but I thought short of that, she would never stop.

I backed away, noticing Paul approaching from his downed position. "You will return to me one day, Hennie. Listen to your friend and let it be before you tarnish what little good is left in our soul."

"Stay away from me. All of you." I looked around the room to the women, who were rousing. "I won't be as forgiving of your betrayal a third time." I walked out—only momentarily obstructed by the two-by-four blocking the door.

CHAPTER 51

THE TWO-BY-FOUR SHATTERED INTO the hallway, surprising Dane. He was panting and sweating as if he had been fighting demons since the moment I left him. He looked over at me and frowned. "What happened?"

I was certain he could sense the power dripping off me. "It was a trap," I summed up.

I realized I could see the shadows of the surrounding demons. My enlightenment had given me new eyes. I wondered what other talents I had. I waved my hand, and the shadows withered into the floor, screeching as they went.

Dane looked at me again. "What happened to you in there?"

"They've turned against me. They tried to kill me." I glanced back at the room. I could see they were all gathering together, discussing the aftermath of their loss. Soon they would be ready for another fight, but I wasn't. "Are you with me, Dane? Or are you with them?"

Dane looked baffled as his eyes darted over mine. "I'm with you."

"Then get me out of here."

Dane didn't waste a moment more to question me about the specifics. He jogged toward me, wrapped his hand in mine, and we ran down the hall, past the infirm patients, down the stairs, and out of the hospital.

On the drive home, I told him everything. I told him of the deceit. I told him how much it hurt me to be rejected again. I told him how good it felt to tell Rachel off once and for all.

He glanced from the road now and then, but didn't say much. When we arrived home, he came around and helped me out of the car. I wasn't feeling any pain, but the tears streaming down my cheeks certainly gave the impression of weakness.

"They won't stop. I know they won't," I rambled as Dane sheltered me under his arm. "They know where I live. We should collect our things and run. At least put some distance between us for now."

Dane nodded. "That's probably for the best."

We reached the stoop and Dane looked around as he usually did for demons that might want to invade my home. I wasn't nearly as worried about it now that I could see them, but habits were hard to break. I stepped inside, counting on my fingers a hundred things I wanted to bring with me, even though I knew I didn't have time for all that. I would be lucky to get a few pairs of underwear and a granola bar for the road.

"I think I have two bags in the closet." I ran down the hall to the coat closet and pulled two small duffle bags out. "Ah-ha!" I ran back and showed Dane. "Found them."

He was still standing in the door, looking inside. He clenched his jaw, but was otherwise calm. "Great, go get us packed. I'll keep watch for them."

I nodded and headed up the stairs. Halfway up, I stopped and looked back. "Dane?"

"What?"

"Come inside."

"Just go. Pack anything for me. I don't want any more surprises."

"I will, but first..." I came back down and stood just inside the door. "...put your foot over the threshold."

Dane stared at me, eyes narrowing slightly. "We don't have time for this."

"Do it."

Dane's jaw tensed again, and he tried to move his foot inside. As if blocked by an imaginary force, he couldn't cross the door jamb. I looked up to an old-school herbal spell hanging over the door. I had reinforced my magical barrier with crude magic to help deter demons drawn in by my hellish power. I never expected the sachet would work. I certainly hadn't predicted who they might need to protect me from.

"Dane?" I whispered as new tears sprang to my eyes. "Do you want to hurt me?"

His eyes glittered over me. Something cold had replaced his usual hungry libido. He no longer wanted my body for sex. "Yes," he answered.

Truth.

I stared at him and him back at me. "Run, Hennie," he whispered. "This spell won't hold me out for long."

I took in a breath, still not wanting to go. I wanted to convince him I was good. That nothing had changed. But apparently it had. I went into that room his lover, but I came out of it, his prey.

"Run!" he bellowed at me.

I turned and ran to the back door. I had nowhere to go, no one to turn to, no one to trust. I was being hunted by my coven, my lover, and the devil himself.

Worse still, I could feel a scratching sensation all up and down my spine. I knew it wasn't just the tickle of fear on the back of my neck. I knew it wasn't the residual magical energy of my run-in with real power.

It was Hennie.

She was scratching her way up to the surface. She wanted out, and I had broken my promise. Now, with the help of the beast she had invited in, they were going to claw their way out of me.

One way or another.

The Devil's Soul
FELICIA JEDLICKA

The Devil's Soul

Book 3 of the Sister Witches

It was a fast fall from grace. Formerly a godly exorcist demoted to the devil's right-hand man, now, Hennie, an unsanctioned creation of the devil's self-loathing, has become a catalyst for a new apocalypse.

As a reformed magic junkie, currently qualifying as a possessor, Hennie is being hunted down. With the help of her ex-boyfriend and the devil herself, her former coven members are set on exorcising her out of this body and back to hell. And apparently, they aren't the only ones.

Enon, self-described as a risen demon—the opposite of a fallen angel—has no desire to save the world from evil. However, he is looking for an evening snack, and earthbound demons are his fa-vorite flavor. Unfortunately, he picked the wrong possessor to mess with.

Thank you so much for reading. I hope you enjoyed the ride and if you aren't getting off here, I encourage you to sign up for my newsletter so I can return your generosity with new release updates and special offers.

Sign-Up

You can also find me on Facebook or visit my website. Keep reading!

Website

Facebook

About the Author

As a Nebraska native, and a small-town girl at that, I have very little to occupy my time beyond imagining a world outside of my own reality. By the grace of God and the seat of my pants, I have kept my waning attention span on the task of becoming an author.

So here I am, an indie author, peddling my words in cyberspace and enduring my comeuppances with an unwavering determination. I may not be a professional, and I certainly am not perfect, but if you've made it this far, you have to admit, this smartass yokel does spin quite a yarn.

From the self-inflicted sweatshop conditions of my unairconditioned childhood home, to the arthritis reaping positions of a sedentary lifestyle, I bring to you: my sarcasm, my oddity, and my heart. Take it with a grain of salt or a teaspoon of sugar, but take it for what it is: a story born of the mind, translated to paper, and gifted to you.

I thank you for your readership and even more for your support. Please recommend this book to your friends and family via any social media that you use. Word of mouth is still the best advertising and is greatly appreciated.

Most importantly, keep reading. I'll keep writing.